RECOLLECTION

THE WORTHINGS

NOELLE ADAMS

1

THE LAST THING I REMEMBER IS THE LOOK ON THE FACE OF my dad in the driver's seat and the sharp curve of the road in the rain.

After that it's only darkness. Like a thick, swirling midnight fog that masks what should be a familiar world.

I wake up knowing my dad is dead. The awareness exists as a weight in my chest, a heaviness in my gut—an old wound that still aches.

My eyes are closed. My head pounds. I shift slightly, trying to move my body into a more comfortable position.

Baby?

The word shudders somewhere in my mind, but I don't hear it. It's only a flicker of a thought. It's not real.

"Scarlett?"

My name. I actually hear it. The voice is low and disembodied. Familiar, although I can't match it with a face.

I should open my eyes. Maybe that will clear the dark fog. I fight to lift my eyelids.

"Scarlett? Wake up. Come back."

The same voice. Low. Male. Slightly husky.

Commanding.

The cold, stark light is blinding when I manage a narrow squint, so I squeeze my eyes back shut.

"Scarlett, open your eyes."

I do what the voice says, then blink several times because the light still hurts.

There's a weird, throaty sound that doesn't make any sense.

When my eyes finally focus, the face looking down at me is the last one I expect. Roughly attractive with dark brown eyes and a dramatic scar slashing down from one ear toward his jaw. Thick, unruly hair that's slightly graying and almost reaches his shoulders.

Arthur Worthing. One of my father's friends. The only one who didn't completely turn against him when the rest of the world did.

I croak, "Mr. Worthing?"

Something odd happens to the face. It tightens visibly. The thin, mobile lips twist. "Scarlett, what's wrong?"

"What the hell is happening here?" I can see beyond his face now. I must be in a hospital room. There's a television bolted to the wall and an ugly, generic cabinet. "My dad?"

"Your... dad?"

"He's..." My throat aches. I swallow hard over a lump that threatens to strangle me. "He's... he's dead."

"Yes. He's dead. For the past six months."

I turn my head away because it feels like I'm going to cry. I don't want Arthur Worthing to see.

After a minute, his last comment penetrates my foggy brain. "Wait. What? Six months? Six *months*?"

Arthur frowns. He's been seated on the edge of a chair pulled up to my bed, leaning over so he's close, but now he straightens up. "Yes. It's been six months since your dad died. You don't..." He clears his throat. "You don't remember?"

"No! Of course I don't remember. It... it just happened, didn't it? The car accident. I remember him going too fast on a curvy road in the rain. Have I been in a coma or something?"

"No. You've been unconscious for a few hours, but the doctor said it was from a concussion. It wasn't a coma. You think the car accident just happened?"

I don't know Arthur all that well. He's been in the background of my life for a long time, but we never interacted in anything more than a cursory way. He's not showing much expression at the moment, but his posture looks stiff. His jaw is working slightly.

He's upset. I'm sure of it.

He's really upset.

My eyes burn, and my throat tightens again. "Didn't it? That's the last thing I remember. The rain and the curve of the road. I know my dad is dead, but I don't remember how I know. It's really been six months? Why are you even here?"

"Why am... I...?" He stands up with a jerky move, his head turned away from me. "I'm going to get the doctor. I'll be right back."

"Okay."

I have no idea what else to say. That dark fog is still swirling in my mind—so many things I should know but don't. My head throbs painfully, and there are lesser aches all over my body.

But none of that matters as much as Arthur Worthing's reaction.

He's always been smart. Aloof. Slightly sarcastic. Completely unflappable.

But he was about to lose it just now, which means something is terribly wrong.

A nurse comes into the room almost immediately and then a doctor several minutes after that.

The doctor has gray hair and a kind face. He shines a light in my eyes, tells me to look in different directions, and then starts asking a series of questions.

"What's your name?"

He has my chart, so he clearly knows who I am. He must be testing to see if I can remember it. "Scarlett Elizabeth Kingston."

"What year is it?"

"It's 2023."

"Do you have any brothers or sisters?"

"No. It's just me and my dad. Or it was. Until he... My mom took off when I was a baby. I never even knew her."

He nods, affirming my answer. For a moment it feels like I did well on a test in school. "And your dad?"

"He's Jack Kingston. The one you've probably heard of."

Anyone who's paid attention to national news in the past year would have heard of Jack Kingston, the supposed financial guru who embezzled millions from his ultra-wealthy clients. He was arrested and convicted, but he fled the country before he could be sent to prison.

"How old are you?" the doctor asks quietly.

Pain flickers briefly in my head as I reach for the answer. "Twenty-seven."

I'm watching the doctor, so I notice when he glances

back to the corner of the room where Arthur retreated after he brought in the nurse.

"Is that wrong?" I ask, trying to straighten up. I don't like lying in bed while everyone else is standing. "If six months have passed, does that mean I'm twenty-eight now?"

I close my eyes, trying to search my mind for all the memories that must be lurking beyond the fog. It hurts my head so much I gasp.

"Yes," the doctor murmurs. "You're twenty-eight."

"I missed my birthday." For some reason, I turn my head to meet Arthur's steady gaze.

His hair is a mess. Sometimes he pulls it back into a low ponytail, but today it's loose, hanging around his face in rumpled waves. His starkly chiseled features are utterly stoic, but there's something in his eyes that's deeply unsettling.

Something akin to grief.

He's basically a stranger to me. We were never close, and I never knew or cared much about him other than the fact that he was my dad's friend and he didn't stop taking my dad's calls when all the shit went down last year. I don't know why I can recognize emotions in his expression that are almost imperceptible.

It makes my stomach churn. I can't stand it. I look back at the doctor's harmless face. "What's going on? Why can't I remember?"

"You've had significant head trauma. Twice in the past six months."

"Twice?"

"The first time in the car accident—the one you remember. And again earlier today." Once more, he glances back toward Arthur.

I turn toward him too, steeling myself against the heavy sensation the man is evoking in me. "Another car accident?"

Arthur shakes his head. "You fell. Off a ladder in my library."

"In your library?" My eyes widen. I know enough about Arthur Worthing to know he lives in a huge estate in northern Virginia, less than an hour from Alexandria. There he houses his family's enormous collection of books and manuscripts. I used to explore the disorganized bookshelves when I was younger, a thrilling and intoxicating undertaking for a bookish girl like me. When I was working on my master's in library science, Arthur gave me access to his set of Louisa May Alcott first editions for my thesis project.

That library was always like a treasure trove to me, so maybe it's not so surprising that I was there earlier today.

Plus that would explain Arthur's inexplicable presence here in the hospital room. He must have been the one to find me after I fell.

"Why was I there?" I ask the question of Arthur since he's the one who must know the answer.

His jaw works visibly for a moment before he answers in an uncharacteristically mild tone. "You've been working for me. Cataloging my library. Ever since your dad died."

My lips part at this new and shocking piece of information.

Closing my eyes again, I once more attempt to pierce the fog to recall events I've clearly lost.

I suck in a sharp breath at the stab through my head. "I can't... I can't remember. Any of it."

"The last thing you remember is the car accident?" The doctor is peering closely at me. I know he saw my wince of pain.

"Yes. Is that normal? I think I remember everything else. All about my childhood and my life and my education and the job I had at the university library and all the shit that happened with my dad. Why is it just the recent stuff that's gone? Is this some kind of amnesia? I thought that only happened in movies."

He chuckles softly at my last comment. "Amnesia is real. But you're right—it doesn't normally look like this. Despite all the medical research that's been done, our brains are still mostly a mystery to us. They do their best to protect us, and that will occasionally manifest itself in unexpected ways. You had two significant head injuries in a relatively short period of time. And you also had significant emotional trauma six months ago. The memory loss could be neurological. Or psychological. Or most likely a combination of the two. We'll do some more tests, of course, but your other responses and what you've articulated so far are otherwise promising for no permanent brain damage."

"So you think I'll get my memory back?"

"I don't know for sure. Every case is different. But often memory loss like this is temporary."

I swallow and relax just a little. I want to look over at Arthur, but his quiet presence is making me nervous, so I don't. "How... How long will it take?"

"I'm afraid I have no idea. Maybe hours. Maybe days. Maybe longer. I wish I could hurry it along for you, but I'm sorry. There's nothing we can do."

Something about the words slices through my consciousness along with another stab of searing pain.

I stifle a whimper and raise my hands to cover my face like I can block out whatever is trying to force its way into my mind.

I sense something in the room. Motion. Tension. I manage to pry my eyes open in time to see the doctor shaking his head in Arthur's direction and then Arthur moving back into the corner where he's been standing.

He'd started moving toward the bed, but the doctor told him not to.

It doesn't make any sense.

I have no idea what's going on with anything anymore.

"What were you doing when your head hurt like that?" the doctor asks softly when the room is still again.

"I was..." I try to catch my breath as I recover from the pain. "I was trying to make myself remember. I felt like I know you... Or I heard you say something similar... Or..." I give up trying to make it make sense.

He meets my eyes steadily. "We have met before. I'm the one who told you that your father died."

There's an image—a moment in the dark of my mind —that's just out of arm's reach. But when I grab for it, I get another one of those stabs of pain. "I can't..." I'm almost crying at the utter frustration of my helplessness. "I can't..."

"Then don't," the doctor says, more firmly than he's been speaking before. "If it hurts when you try to remember, then don't."

"But I need to—"

"When it comes back to you, it will be when your brain is ready for it. Forcing it before your brain has recovered might end up doing more damage. I can't imagine how hard it is for you not to be able to remember, but I think slow and easy is the best way to proceed here. Your brain is doing its job to the best of its ability right now. It's trying to protect you by holding back those memories. So let it. You'll remember when your brain has healed."

I nod mutely, too emotional to speak but not wanting either of the men in the room to see it.

"We're going to let you rest for a little while now. Then we'll get some people in to do some more tests to see if we can get more information to work with. For now, though, don't force it. If it hurts to think about something, don't make yourself think about it. Powering through isn't the way to go here."

I nod again. Gulp and hope I'm not going to burst into tears.

The doctor turns toward Arthur and makes a silent gesture with his head. Arthur follows him out.

They have a conversation right outside the door, but they're talking too low for me to hear.

I'd strain to listen, but I can't right now. All I can do is cry.

Two days later, Arthur pulls up in his fancy dark blue SUV to the front of the hospital and jumps out to help me into the front seat.

I don't need help. I have no broken bones. Only a few minor bruises. And my mind is working fine for all basic functions. I can walk and eat and dress myself and read and move around just fine.

The only thing missing is my memory of the past six

months.

The past two days have been full of tests and examinations. From my original doctor and also two more specialists that Arthur called in to give second and third opinions, one remotely and one in person. The other doctors agreed with the initial conclusion. Give my brain time to heal. Surround myself with settings and routines that should be familiar even if they aren't now. Don't try to force the memories to return. If something makes my head hurt, stop doing it. Get a lot of rest.

So basically there's nothing I can do to fix myself other than wait it out.

Even though my body is working fine, I let Arthur ease me into the front seat because he wants to and it's easier to just let him.

I've never been a particularly feisty person. My dad used to tease me about how I exist in a cloud of docility that masks an unbendable, stubborn streak.

He was right about me, but I'm not going to get stubborn about something so silly. Arthur is worried. He feels responsible for me. He's evidently been my employer, and he was my dad's only friend at the end. I don't have anyone else. I had to give up all but one of my friends when I stood by my father.

If Arthur wants to put his hand on my back to support me as I climb into the SUV, that's fine with me.

I thank the orderly who pushed me out in the wheelchair and settle myself in the seat. I grab for the seat belt automatically and reach down to adjust the position of the seatback.

I know where both of them are. Acting on instinct, I open the console compartment between the seats and pull out a bottle of fancy water.

No doubt I've been in this car before. Many times.

But I don't remember any of them.

"You okay?" Arthur asks softly when he's back behind the steering wheel. His eyes are the warm color of dark chocolate, and they're focused on my face with an unnerving scrutiny.

"Yeah. Fine. It's just... unsettling."

"I can only imagine. Please let me know what you need, and I'll do it."

I gulp. The mild offer feels like a weight in my gut, and I have no idea why. Instead of finding the appropriate words, I nod.

He pulls away from the hospital entrance and drives in silence until he's merged onto the highway that leads out of Alexandria. The Worthing estate is about forty minutes to the west.

I've been there many times. The mansion and grounds are familiar to me in a way that Arthur himself isn't. And evidently it's been my residence for six months now, but I can't imagine it feeling like home.

"You're sure you don't want to stay with Jenna for a

while?" Arthur asks, finally breaking the silence.

He might have been reading my mind.

Jenna is my best friend, and she lives in North Carolina. All my other friends dropped me when I left the country with my father, but Jenna never did and we've stayed in daily touch. Arthur evidently knows she's my only close relationship anymore. He called her the day I was injured, and I've talked to her several times since. She wanted to drive the six hours to see me right away, but she has a job and a family, and she has to make arrangements before she visits. She's planning to come see me soon.

I could have gone to stay with her. Part of me wants to, but I want to get my memory back even more.

"The doctor said I should go home. Be in familiar surroundings. If I've been living at your place, then that's where I should go."

"Yes. I agree. But you don't have to come immediately. If you're not comfortable with me—"

"It's not you." It's partly him—for some reason, the quiet, intelligent authority he exudes disturbs me unduly —but he hasn't done anything wrong. Everything he's said and done for the past two days has been thoughtful and polite and respectful. Kind of aloof. He's not sharing anything about himself even when I ask directly. But he's been good to me, and I assume it's based on nothing except loyalty to my father. "Thank you for all your help. I really think I'll feel unsettled and uncomfortable right now wherever I go. Even at Jenna's. It's the situation. It's not you."

He inclines his head in a brief nod, his eyes focused mostly on the road and only occasionally darting over to my face.

"How did it happen?" I ask, finding the silence more uncomfortable than conversation. "How did I start working for you after Dad died?"

His jaw works slightly. "What do you remember?"

"I remember everything before the car accident. I think. I remember our life in the Caribbean." When Dad had to flee his conviction, he convinced me to leave the country with him and live on a private island off of Cuba to avoid prison. I'd had a good job in a university library in Charlotte and was starting to build a career for myself and a real social circle for the first time in my life.

But my dad was my only family, and I chose him instead.

I was wrong. It was a mistake. I could have loved him without giving up everything. But no matter how much he loved me, he was always selfish at heart and he didn't want to be alone. So the worst, loneliest months of my life were the ones I spent in exile with him.

I clear my throat. "He thought he could fix things. He wouldn't tell me how. But that's why he was so insistent on coming back that week." I peer over at Arthur's face. "You know what he was doing here, don't you?"

He meets my eyes briefly but doesn't answer.

"Was he trying to bribe people in DC?"

"Yes. I told him not to. It wasn't worth the risk, and it wasn't going to work. But he thought he'd ruined your life. He was right. He had."

"It was my choice."

"Yes. But it wasn't a free choice. You loved him, and he used that love to manipulate you."

It hurts to hear the words, but not as much as I would have expected. I must have somehow worked through much of this in the six months I can't remember. "Yes. He did. I didn't know it at the time, but he did."

"He knew it too. He managed to smother his conscience a lot of the time, but he did have one. He wanted to fix things for you. I told him coming here would only make things worse, but he was desperate."

"I remember him telling me someone was coming after him and we needed to get away." The image of that terrible night plays vividly through my mind like a bleak suspense movie. "I remember it was raining and he was racing for the airport. I remember him missing the curve in the road. I remember his face." I twist my hands together in my lap. "That's it. After that, it's just blank."

"Your dad died in the wreck. You were bruised up and had a concussion, but you weren't seriously injured. You didn't have anywhere to go afterward. You gave up your apartment when you ran away with him, and Charlotte was too far away anyway. So you came back to my place, planning to stay only until you recovered and made a plan for your life. When I offered you the job cataloging my library, you took it because it gave you some breathing room and time to figure out what you wanted to do."

I think about this for a long time. It makes sense. I can see how it happened. After a couple of minutes, I turn to look at his unreadable expression. "Thank you. For helping me out. I must have felt... helpless. Completely alone."

"You did. And you were worried that returning to Charlotte and your old friends would put them in an awkward situation since everyone hated your dad so much."

A faint thread of amusement tickles me. I breathe out a laugh. "I guess I didn't mind putting you in an awkward situation."

His mouth quirks up just slightly. "No. You didn't mind. I already faced some of it because I didn't break all ties with your dad."

"Why did you—?" I cut off my own question, not sure it's appropriate for the nature of our relationship.

He must know what I was going to ask. "I don't have many friends. I was a lonely rich boy—a typical cliché, I guess. But even as an adult, most of my acquaintances have been superficial. Your dad reached out to me. I knew immediately what his game was. I've always had good instincts about that kind of thing. He accepted my no without any resentment and didn't stop being friendly. I liked that about him."

"Yeah." I close my eyes, picturing my dad's face and smiling. "He couldn't hold a grudge to save his life. And he really liked you. He would talk about how you weren't fake at all and having a conversation with you was like going to college."

"I'm not sure that's a compliment."

I laugh softly. "It was from him."

"I've had this..." He gestures toward the scar on his face. "Since I was thirteen. It taught me that much of the world values the superficial more than anything else. Your dad was one of the few who really tried to look beyond the surface with me."

The words linger in the air of the car. Surrounding me. Filling me. Touching my heart. "Yeah."

"That doesn't excuse what your dad did, but I don't much care what the rest of the world thinks about me. I managed to stay his friend while drawing boundaries about never helping him break the law or hurt other people—including you. But he'd actually been asking for my help in getting you into a better position, so I'd already come up with the job possibility for you, even before the car accident."

My heart does a funny little jump. "So my dad was trying to find me a job?"

"Yes. He saw what a mistake he'd made with you and was desperate to give you a way out. He wasn't a good man. We both know that. But he also wasn't a monster, and you were his priority in his final days, Scarlett."

I swallow over a tightness in my throat. Take a few deep breaths. "Thank you. For telling me that. And for trying to help back then. And for helping me now."

"You're welcome."

There's nothing else I can think of to say, and I'm too emotional to say it anyway. We drive in silence for half an hour. I lean my head back and close my eyes, pretending to be asleep.

When the car slows down, I open my eyes, needing to see what's going on. We've pulled off the highway and onto a two-lane road. We follow this road for about ten more minutes until we reach the Worthing estate.

It feels like my hair is messy from leaning it against the headrest, so I pull down the visor mirror to check. My medium-brown hair is straight and longer than I remember. It's well past my shoulders now. I smooth down a few flyaways. My eyes are brown too—more amber than Arthur's chocolate brown. My features are regular. Nothing special. My eyebrows really need plucking, and there's still a visible bruise on one side of my forehead and cheekbone.

With a sigh, I flip the visor back up and glance over to

discover Arthur was watching me peer at myself. "Still me," I say wryly.

"Yes. You are."

There's an edge of texture in his final word that makes my chest clench. His face works very briefly before it settles back into his normal aloof composure.

"What is it?" I blurt out.

"What is what?"

"What's going on? It feels like there are all these secrets you aren't telling me. You aren't... You aren't acting like you used to with me. What's going on? Please tell me!"

"All the doctors have said you're supposed to remember naturally. We can't force you."

"I know what they said, but it's not fair to leave me in the dark. It feels like I'm... I'm floundering. Why are you acting...?" I suck in a hoarse gasp. "Why are you acting weird?"

His jaw tenses again. He's staring ahead at the curvy road. He takes a few breaths so thick I can hear them.

"Please."

He gives his head a little shake and turns back to meet my gaze, says in his natural voice, "There aren't big secrets. This is strange and difficult for me too. You've been living and working with me for six months. We... We got to know each other. I was very worried when I found you on the floor of the library. And I'm still worried for you now. I know I'm not the one going through it like you are, but this isn't entirely easy for me either. If you're picking up on odd nuances, that's probably what they are."

"Oh." I pause. Think. I never imagined actually being Arthur Worthing's friend. "So we were... We were... friendly?"

He inclines his head slightly in that short nod he uses a lot.

"Oh." I shift in my seat, feeling the most ridiculous flutter of pleasure.

Pleasure.

Where it came from, I have no idea.

"Did I call you Arthur?"

He exhales in dry amusement. "You did."

"Oh." I lick my lips, trying to make sense of that new information. "Well, I believe you. And I appreciate that this must be kind of hard for you. I wish I could... I wish I could jump back to however we were interacting before, but I'm sorry. I don't remember any of it." My voice cracks slightly.

"I know you don't."

There's a bittersweet note in the words that makes my heart ache again, but I have to shake the feeling away.

It's too much. I simply can't deal with anything other than getting through this one day.

Whatever friendship we developed in the past six months has been scattered into the dark swirl of fog in my mind. It simply doesn't exist anymore.

2

NEVILLE WORTHING AMASSED A FORTUNE IN SHIPPING AND transport in the nineteenth century and in 1887 built a sprawling, over-the-top mansion in northern Virginia horse country.

The fortune has been divided between Worthing descendants all over the world, but in pure patriarchal style, the estate has been passed down from oldest son to oldest son until Arthur inherited it when his father died fifteen years ago.

Arthur lives in the east wing, and the rest of the mansion is closed off—far too expansive and expensive to clean, maintain, furnish, and heat. When my father and I visited in the past, I would sneak away to explore. It always felt like I'd walked into *The Secret Garden*. A huge house and grounds, much of it dusty and untended with hidden nooks and secrets skulking behind every shadow.

I have a glimmer of the same feeling today as I let Arthur help me out of the front seat of the SUV and stare up at the chateauesque structure with its steep, gabled roofs and ornate towers with spires.

Glancing over, I notice Arthur watching me closely. I smile. "It's always been kind of excessive, hasn't it?"

He chuckles dryly. "That's putting it kindly. It's a ridiculous monstrosity."

His expression flickers with something like affection. I suddenly realize that, despite its outlandishness, he loves this house.

My realization humanizes him. So much so that my stomach twists. He's not just a brilliant, isolated, standoffish friend of my father's. He's a man who loves his home.

His forehead creases with a frown. "What's wrong?"

"Nothing." I start up the wide steps leading to the front door. It's silly to let something so insignificant affect me. I've got more important things to focus on than Arthur.

We're greeted at the door by a plump, attractive woman in her fifties with silvering hair and blue eyes. She smiles at me warmly and reaches out to squeeze my upper arm. "We're so glad to have you back, dear. We were so worried."

"Thank you." I smile back, recognizing Stella as Arthur's longtime housekeeper but not expecting such an effusive welcome. "I'm doing okay, considering. I'm so sorry I can't remember anything about living here recently."

"I know. Arthur called to let us know. What you need is rest. Soon you'll be back to yourself." She sounds so kind and so confident that my throat tightens up.

I hope what she's saying is true, but I have no way of knowing for sure. "Thank you."

"Come on to your room. Billy will carry your things."

Billy is Stella's husband. He takes care of routine maintenance and manages the grounds. The two of them are Arthur's live-in domestic staff, and they bring in extra help for large jobs when they need to.

My rooms are on the second floor at the end of the hall. It's a large suite with a high ceiling, luxurious bathroom, cozy sitting area, and a huge four-poster bed with a gauzy canopy.

It's gorgeous. I'm gazing around in pleasure when I notice Arthur peering at me again.

He's standing completely still, not moving a muscle, and his dark eyes are focused on my face. There's nothing evident in his expression to provide a clue, but I'm sure he's watching, waiting, almost holding his breath.

I realize why. He's wondering if I'll recognize something. If it will start to bring back more memories.

I love these rooms, but I don't think I've ever seen them before in my life.

"This is beautiful," I say mildly. "Thank you."

If someone can slump without making a single move, Arthur does. He gives me that slight nod. "I'll let you get settled. Feel free to go anywhere you want in the east wing, but I'd rather you not venture into the rest of the house without someone with you. It's in disrepair, and I can't vouch for its safety."

"Understood. I'll stay in this section. Is it okay for me to wander around in the gardens?"

"Of course. This is your home." He clears his throat. "It was your home."

My laptop is resting on a small writing desk near a window. I walk over to run my fingers over the closed top. One of my cardigan sweaters is draped over the chair.

This is my stuff. I did live here. I must have felt at home.

I have no idea how.

"Thank you." I'm not sure what else to say to Arthur, who is still lingering, watching me in that unnerving way he has.

He murmurs thickly as he starts to leave, "You don't have to thank me again."

I spend the remainder of the day resting and wandering around aimlessly, hoping for something to trigger a memory. I'm so uncomfortable and anxious that I accept Stella's offer to bring dinner up to my room and eat alone, watching an old television show I like on my phone.

It's better than trying to make polite conversation with Arthur.

The following day, my friend Jenna comes up to see me from Charlotte. When I ask Arthur about a good nearby hotel for her, he insists that she stay here with us.

It's an immense relief to see someone I know and love —someone I'm certain of my relationship to. We hang out and have lunch at the estate but then go shopping in the afternoon.

Jenna was in graduate school with me, but she got married early and already has three children. She's one of those warm, outgoing, nurturing people I've always been drawn toward. Basically the exact opposite of me. She makes conversation easy in a weird situation, telling me everything that's happened to her and her family in the past six months and then asking about how things have gone since I woke up in the hospital.

She doesn't ask anything harder until we're browsing through shoes in a department store. "So does it feel like your dad just died to you?"

I pause, surprised by the question but not upset. "No. It really doesn't. I'm not sure why since I don't remember anything after it happened. Don't get me wrong. It still hurts. When I think about it in a focused way, I'll definitely start crying. But it doesn't feel... new. It doesn't make any sense."

"The whole thing is kind of crazy, but I guess our minds do crazy things sometimes. At least you don't have to go through all the stages of grief again. That would be terrible."

"I know. Had I... Had I resolved things? About my dad?"

She picks up a pair of high-heeled boots and admires them. "Yes. I think so. You were getting there. You'd been going to counseling, which I think was helping. It was hard —because you were so conflicted. Your dad wasn't the easiest person to love."

"Yeah. That I do remember. I was really angry with him —for pushing me into giving up my whole life to run away with him. But it feels like a lot of that is settled too. I don't get so angry when I think about it now."

"You'd worked through a lot of it."

"No matter what he did, it was my decision. I didn't have to go with him."

"No, you didn't. As I told you many times."

"I should have listened to you. I was stupid."

Jenna reaches over and rubs my shoulder. "You made a mistake, but you loved your dad. Love makes us do all kinds of stupid things."

"I guess." I wander over toward the purses, seeing a small satchel I like the looks of. "Sometimes I wonder what my life would be like if I'd stayed put. Kept my job and my apartment. Maybe I'd be married to Carl."

Carl was the guy I was dating at the time. We weren't serious, but it felt like there might have been potential. I lost him with everything else, and the truth is other losses were a lot harder.

"I doubt it. He was too nice for you. You need more of a challenge."

I make a face. "I don't know why. A nice, simple guy sounds pretty good to me right now."

Jenna snorts and changes the subject. "So how are things with Arthur?"

"What do you mean?"

"I mean are you getting along okay? Is it weird? You didn't know him very well six months ago, and now he's... there."

I keep looking at the purse, opening the zipper pockets and inspecting the lining, needing the slight distraction it provides. "It's very weird if you want to know the truth. He said we became friends. *Friends*. With Arthur Worthing. It's... weird."

"He seems like a decent guy."

"I think he is. It's just that he's always been my dad's friend. Not mine."

"He was younger than your dad."

"Sure. But he's still got to be almost twenty years older than me. And he's one of those people who never lets anyone else in. He doesn't open up, and he doesn't let me see what he's thinking."

I say the words instinctively since that's always been my impression of the man. But I suddenly realize he *has* opened up to me—at least a little—in the past couple of days. That conversation in the car yesterday felt almost deep, and it revealed a lot about Arthur's character that I hadn't known before.

Maybe he isn't who I've always assumed.

I clear my throat. "Anyway, he's basically a stranger, and there I am, living in his house."

"Maybe you can get to know him again."

"Maybe. But is it worth the trouble? I'm not sure that I'm going to stay there for very long. He won't let me do any work in the library yet, but surely there's not that much left to do if I've been working for six months. I'll try to finish it up, and then I can find a real job—maybe closer to you—and try to start my life again."

"Is that what you want?"

"I think so. What else can I do?"

"I don't know." Jenna's expressive face twists like something is upsetting her. "Maybe you'll get your memory back."

"Maybe. But I haven't gotten even a flicker yet, and it's been three days. I might need to settle my mind around the possibility of never getting those six months back." I sigh. "I guess it wouldn't be the end of the world."

"A lot can happen in six months. It would be a shame to lose it forever. So maybe don't give up yet."

"I'm not giving up yet. I'm trying to be realistic. And life sometimes takes things away without ever giving back."

We shop for a few more hours, then get manicures, then eat dinner out, so it's late by the time we return. Arthur is working in his home office, so I stop by to check in and say good night. Not because I want to see him but because it seems polite.

He asks how my day went and says he's glad I had a good time. I linger for a minute in the doorway, feeling like I should say more but having no idea what.

He doesn't say anything either. Just looks at me. So I give up and say good night with a superficial smile before I make a getaway.

Jenna has to leave the following morning. We have breakfast in her room, and then I take a short walk while she showers, dresses, and gets her stuff ready. When I return to the house, I can't find her. She's not in her room, she's not in my room, and she's not in the main entry hall or the sitting room. I wander down the first-floor hallway and glance into Arthur's office since the door is mostly open.

Jenna is in there, talking to Arthur. They're both standing up, him behind his desk and Jenna not too far away from him. They're talking with a quiet intensity that's evident even from my distance.

I can hear the murmur of their voices but not the exact words. Jenna looks almost angry, and Arthur's expression is set, stubborn.

They're arguing. That much is clear. I strain to hear the words, but the only thing I can catch is Jenna saying, "It's not fair to her. It's not *fair*."

Well, they're obviously talking about me.

I can't just stand here, trying to eavesdrop. I swing the door to make a sound.

They break off, both of them taking steps back and turning toward the doorway.

"Hey. Sorry," Jenna says, flushed and sheepish.

"What's going on?" I frown as I look between her and Arthur.

His face has settled back into its cool composure, revealing almost nothing. "I believe Jenna is ready to go."

I scowl at him since this is clearly an attempt to fob off my question. "What were you arguing about?"

"We weren't arguing," Jenna says. "Just talking. Come on. I've got to get going soon."

I'm about to protest but then decide I'll have better

luck getting information if Arthur isn't in the room. I can usually convince Jenna to tell me the truth. So with one last glance at Arthur's unmoving face, I walk with Jenna out of the office and then toward the front door, where she left her overnight bag.

She picks it up, and we walk outside.

"Tell me what's going on," I grit out.

"It's really nothing. It probably looked weirder than it really is. I was just asking him about what the doctor said about your memory. How much we should tell you about what you missed in the past six months."

"It looked like more than that."

"He doesn't want me to give you details. About things that happened. And that's hard—not being able to tell you about things that happened to you."

"What things?"

She shrugs. "Anything. He wants to follow the doctor's advice to the letter and let you remember things naturally. I know he's probably right. We don't want to do more damage. But it just seems..." Her features contort like she's about to cry. "It's hard."

Now I'm about to cry too. I lean over to hug her. "It really is. The whole thing sucks. But if there's something you want to tell me, you can tell me. I should be the one to decide how much information is shared with me. Arthur doesn't get to decide. He has no claim on me."

Jenna's shoulders shake slightly as we hug. She's really

upset right now. Maybe even more than me. "I guess not," she says raspily. "But he might be right. Let's give it a little time and see if things come back naturally."

"Okay. There can't be that much to tell me anyway. It sounds like I've been here most of the time, working in the library. How much could have happened to me all by myself in this old place?"

Jenna gives a shaky laugh. "Exactly. There's not that much to tell."

That night I don't sleep well, tossing and turning and waking up every hour with a racing heart and panting breath. I'm pretty sure I dream, but I don't remember any of the images. Nothing but intense sensations of fear and restlessness and longing.

It's almost two when I give up on sleeping and get up, sliding on the old fuzzy slippers I've had for far too long.

I need to walk. Breathe different air. Think about something other than these shadowed, chaotic visions.

The house is silent. Arthur, Stella, and Billy turned in long ago and are no doubt asleep in their beds like normal people at this time of night. The hallways and stairs aren't pitch-black because a few strategic lights are left burning. There's still something almost creepy about the big old house, wide halls, and ornamental furnishings as I pass through. During the day, they're familiar. At night, I might as well be the heroine of a Gothic novel.

Without making a conscious decision, I end up in the library, which is in the east wing at the end of the ground-floor hallway. The room has been familiar to me for a long time, but it still strikes me like something from a fairy tale. Mahogany bookshelves line every wall, extending all the way up to the high ceilings. In addition to an enormous desk near the bay window, there are also cozy reading nooks scattered around, including my favorite curtained window seat.

I wander over to it now, looking out at the sprawling gardens and yards still lit dimly by landscape lighting.

Over the past two days, I've studied the work I did during these six months. There's still more to do, but I clearly developed a practical, organized catalog system for the Worthing collection. In addition to the information on the computer, there are notes on index cards in my hand-writing.

It's my work. So much of it. But I can't remember doing any of it.

"Why the hell aren't you in bed?"

The gruff question from the doorway behind me startles me so much I jump and whirl around.

Arthur is stepping into the library, wearing blue cotton pajama pants and a white T-shirt. His slippers are as old as mine, and his hair is a tangled mess. He's never been a particularly dapper dresser—he normally wears trousers and an oxford with the sleeves rolled to just below his elbow—but I've never seen him so undone before.

It has the strangest effect on me. My cheeks flush, and something deep and heavy clenches below my belly. It's not lust as I understand it. It's more like... ownership.

He's scowling, obviously unaware of the effect his appearance is having on me. "It's two in the morning. You should be asleep."

"So should you." Ever since I woke up in the hospital, I've treated Arthur with the polite passivity I naturally fall back on to interact with the world. But my reply right now is sharp. Tart.

"I don't have a head injury. You do. The doctor said you need rest more than anything else."

"I know what the doctor said." His grumpiness is starting to bug me. He's acting like he has some sort of say in the choices I make for my own life. "But I also know that I'm the one who makes decisions for me. Do you really think if I was able to sleep, I'd be up in the middle of the night right now?"

My salty tone surprises him. His eyes widen. His brows pull together. "Are you okay?"

"I'm fine. I just couldn't sleep. It happens sometimes. I don't need you rousted out of your bed to growl at me like a bear coming out of hibernation."

His mouth twitches up just a little.

"Are you actually laughing at me right now?"

"I'm not laughing."

"It sure looks like you are." Other than the brief lip quirk, there's no sign in his expression that he's amused. But I can see that he is. His eyes have warmed, his features softened.

"I haven't seen you get annoyed with me since the hospital."

I frown. "I've been annoyed with you."

"Have you? Because you've been treating me with that empty courtesy you show to strangers. I was afraid I was stuck with that from you forever."

I'm not sure why his words fire me up—he's not insulting me in any way—but they do. "I've been trying to be nice! That's what any decent person would do."

"I don't want nice from you, Scarlett." There's the slightest hint of texture in his voice.

It makes me shiver, but I hide the reaction. "Then what exactly do you want?"

"I want you to be yourself." He's still standing across the room, not moving any closer.

"This is myself. Believe it or not, I'm a nice person. I like being agreeable and polite and not getting into point-less arguments about ridiculous things. I'm not a loud, opinionated person."

"You are opinionated. You have all kinds of opinions

about almost everything. You just don't want to share them with other people."

"What's wrong with that?"

"Because the real Scarlett is in there, hiding under the surface." He finally comes closer, lifting one hand like he's going to touch me but then dropping it again. "She's who I want to see."

I'm breathless again—not from surprise or annoyance this time. I stare up at him with wide eyes and hot cheeks. "Did I... Did I... Did you see her before?"

He opens his mouth to reply. I see the answer on his lips. But then he jerks his head to the side and swallows visibly.

"Arthur?" It feels like the first time I've ever called him by his first name, although I know it's not.

All the intensity that's been vibrating inside him disperses as he lets out a long breath. "I caught a glimpse a time or two," he says mildly. "We weren't strangers, and that's how you're treating me now."

"I know. I'm sure it's very weird for you. But I don't remember any of that. It's not... it's not personal. I'm doing the best I can."

"I know you are. You're doing just fine."

His words make me feel better. I don't want to hurt his feelings or offend him by not remembering our becoming friends before, and he appears to understand that.

But I also feel something akin to disappointment, loss.

Because the angst I sensed in him a minute ago was real, and his mild composure right now is his way of hiding, as much as my polite passivity.

This is safer. Far safer. But it does feel like I'm not getting everything.

Arthur gives his head a little shake like he's brushing off lingering tendrils of emotion. "Well, since you can't sleep, do you want some hot chocolate?"

My lips part. "Yes. That's exactly what I want."

"I could use some too. Come on."

I follow him out of the library, down the hall, through the dining room, and into the kitchen. There he takes the milk out of the commercial-size refrigerator and pours some into a saucepan.

I go to the pantry to get the cocoa and sugar, bringing them to the counter next to the stove.

Only then do I wonder how I knew exactly where they were.

"Have we done this before?" I ask softly as he idly stirs the milk as it warms.

All he says is "Yes."

I don't say anything as he adds the cocoa and sugar until it's dissolved and the liquid is hot. Then he pours it into two mugs.

We carry our drinks back into the library and sit in the window seat to drink.

There's a lot going on behind his silence and his stoic

expression. He has stormy depths that are both fascinating and unnerving. But he seems determined to not let me see them.

It's not like I can blame him. I don't want him to see into my mind and heart either.

"I didn't expect you to wear pajamas like that," I blurt out after several minutes. Then I flush when I realize what I said.

His thick eyebrows arch. His lips twitch up in that appealing way I've only seen a couple of times. "Did you assume I sleep naked?"

I really don't need that visual. He's not any sort of bodybuilder, but he's got long limbs and broad shoulders and the utilitarian kind of fitness of a man who lives an active life. His naked body will be attractive. I know it for sure.

"No. I was thinking more of satin pajamas and a velvet smoking jacket. Maybe a pipe."

He chokes on a stifled laugh.

It feels like a victory.

"I bet you don't even have silk sheets," I add.

"Sorry to disappoint you. Too slippery."

"I've always thought so too. I like thick, soft cotton."

He nods. "Exactly right."

I feel like beaming but have no idea why. I hide the expression behind my mug.

After a moment of emotional pleasure, I start feeling

awkward about it. I used to sometimes feel this way on dates that were going really well. It's been a long time since I experienced it, and I never felt that way about Arthur.

It doesn't seem... appropriate. He's a friend of my father's and nothing else to me. Maybe the head injury messed up my natural responses.

To hide my discomfort, I say the first thing that pops into my head (another thing I rarely do). "You were a cute little boy."

Arthur blinks.

Well, shit. That random comment did absolutely nothing to ease the awkwardness.

"Sorry. I was looking around in here this afternoon and found an old photo album. There were pictures of you in it."

"I'm sure you had better things to do than look at old pictures of me." His tone is very dry, but he doesn't sound annoyed. Maybe slightly self-conscious.

"Yeah, it wasn't like I was searching for them. But I thought they were cute." I get up and wander over to the shelf where I found the album. I carry it back over to where we've been sitting and leaf through the pages until I find the photos. I can't help but smile as I look down again at the ultra-serious expression on the dark-haired, dark-eyed boy in every single pose.

He makes a huffing sound as he leans over to look too.

"Didn't you ever smile?" I ask, gently stroking the small

face with my fingertip. Something inside me wants to ease the expression into a wide smile.

"Sure. But these were the formal photos for posterity. I hated them. I had to sit for hours and not mess up my hair and clothes."

"Oh, I guess that makes sense. So you didn't always look like this?" The little boy in the photograph appears to be carrying the weight of the world at no more than ten years old.

When Arthur doesn't answer, I dart a quick look over at him. His eyes are focused slightly past my face, like he's trapped in a thought he doesn't know what to do with.

"Arthur?" My voice breaks. "Were you always this unhappy?" I don't know why it matters so much to me, but it does.

He gives his head a quick shake. "Of course not."

"Do you have any pictures of when you were happy?"

He opens his mouth, then closes it again. Finally says, "I... don't think so. My mom had some, I'm sure, but they would have disappeared along with all the rest of her stuff after she died." He says the words lightly, as if they don't mean much.

I gulp. "When did your mom die?"

"I was twelve."

"Were you happy when it was just you and her?"

This question appears to surprise him. He thinks about it for a minute before responding. "Yes. My dad would travel sometimes for business. Those were the best days. She would relax. We would get food out—like fast food or ice cream or whatever—and watch movies." He almost smiles. "I was happy then."

I reach out to touch his arm very lightly. "I'm glad you had at least that."

We sit in silence, not looking at each other, until the emotional tension has eased. I flip through some of the earlier pages of the album, and we chat about some of his ancestors.

I'm giggling over his description of his grandfather when I glance over and catch his gaze lower than my face. A quick look down at myself highlights the fact that I'm wearing nothing but a thin white nightgown—a pretty, faintly vintage one with crocheted lace around the scooped neckline. I must have bought it in the past six months because I have no idea where it came from.

Last night I thought it was pretty, so I put it on.

I've got a compact, curvy body—nothing all that special—but the curve of my breasts and the peaks of my nipples are visible right now beneath the soft fabric.

I flush again, hotly this time and paired with a clench of excitement between my legs.

What the hell?

I'm clearly all screwed up in the head if I'm getting turned on by a stray look from Arthur Worthing.

Completely inappropriate. On so many levels.

I drop my eyes and lick my lips until I realize what I'm doing. "Well, I guess I'll try to get some sleep. Thanks for the hot chocolate."

"You're welcome."

I wish his voice wasn't quite so thick. It's giving me naughty thoughts.

His mug is empty, so I take it from his hand. "I'll put these up. Good night."

"Good night." He doesn't move. He's not stiff or tense. Just motionless.

I have no idea what to say or do, so I get out of there.

Fast.

3

_____

PAST

FOR THE FIRST FOUR WEEKS AFTER MY DAD DIES, I DO almost nothing except work and sleep and cry.

The job Arthur offered me in his library is a godsend. It provides safety, isolation, and enough distraction for me to not crawl into bed and never come out. I can spend all day focused on books and be tired enough to sleep most nights.

I gave up the life I used to have for my father. Without him, I have absolutely nothing. No family. No home. No support. No money since the assets he was hiding have been discovered and now frozen.

Nothing except a lot of regrets and a lot of memories. And this library.

Arthur Worthing moves quietly through the periphery of my days, always busy with his own comings and goings and seldom venturing into the foreground of my attention.

He feels sorry for me. That's why he's helping me out and letting me stay. That and lingering loyalty to my father. I hate being an object of sympathy, but Arthur never appears to feel anything deeply, so even his pity is probably nothing more than an occasional passing thought.

Gradually I've fallen into a hazy emotional stupor that is much more palatable than the wrenching grief and undirected anger that slammed me in the first few days.

This is okay. This is better. At least this lethargic fog doesn't threaten to consume me.

I can live like this for a while. Maybe a long while. Maybe forever.

It's better than the roller coaster of my life before.

Late one afternoon, just over a month after the car accident that changed everything, I'm in my normal position behind the big desk, searching for information on the volume of Thomas Carlyle's essays that sits in front of me. There are thousands of books in this library. For each one, I need to archive the publication information and then do research on the value and provenance of the volume. The Worthing collection includes priceless first editions but also countless books that look old and fancy but are actually worthless reprints.

Arthur doesn't want to purge the library. He's keeping everything. But he needs to know which books are valuable and which aren't.

This Carlyle is only eighty years old—one of those leather-bound editions intended for display on an impressive-looking bookshelf rather than for reading. It's neither rare nor special, although I do love the feel of the leather under my fingertips.

Oddly, the book reminds me of Arthur. Smooth and cool and dignified on the surface but with messy edges and the occasional page torn from age.

The metaphor amuses me. I almost smile as I stroke the frayed page edges, wondering if Arthur's too-long, rumpled hair might feel similar.

I wonder why he doesn't keep it shorter. It's not like he's an old man—he was several years younger than my father, so he can't be older than his late forties—but he exudes dignity and professionalism. The hair simply doesn't fit the image.

"Is it a good book?"

The voice from the doorway shocks me. I straighten up with a jerk, blushing like I was caught doing something naughty.

"I'm sorry," he says, striding into the room. He's wearing dark gray trousers and a blue shirt, well-tailored but open at the collar and rolled up at the sleeves. "Did I startle you?"

"Yes, you startled me! You almost gave me a heart attack. Haven't you ever heard of knocking?" I sound way too bad-tempered. I'm not even sure where it's come from. I just don't want him intruding on my private thoughts.

His expression is surprised but curious rather than annoyed at my implication that he's not allowed to venture unchallenged into a room in his own house. "You were smiling down at the book. I was wondering if it was something good."

"Oh. No. Not really. Just a pretentious reprint from the forties. And, sure, Carlyle had a certain sense of humor, but I don't exactly look to him for comedy."

"No. I wouldn't think so."

I have absolutely no doubt that Arthur has read and is familiar with Thomas Carlyle. He's not simply trying to look smart. He never earned more than an undergraduate degree, but he's still one of the most well-read and educated men I've ever met.

When I was seventeen, I came here for a visit with my dad, and Arthur had a ten-minute conversation with me about Jane Austen, who I was reading. I came away convinced he was the smartest man in the world, and I nursed a short-lived crush on him because of it.

I had crushes on almost everyone back then, so it didn't

mean anything. The daydreams were quickly drowned by romantic fantasies about younger, better-looking men.

But I get a flicker—just the faintest flicker—of a similar feeling right now as he lowers his long length into the upholstered side chair by the desk. He's got his hair pulled back at the nape of his neck, but a few strands have come loose and even the ponytail doesn't look sleek and neat. The thick waves of brown hair are threaded with gray and seem to defy any attempt to restrain them.

He's got dark hair on his forearms and a big, expensive watch on his left wrist. A large gold ring with an emerald set in an engraving of his family crest. The scar slashing down one side of his face is old. White. Dramatic.

He's had it from the first time I ever saw him. I wonder how he got it. I used to ask my dad, but he didn't know and said Arthur never told anyone.

I'm suddenly aware of him as a human being. Not just a figment of my past or an accessory to my father or a one-dimensional figure to be compared to an old book. A real-life, breathing human being. Solid. Strong. Masculine. Deep.

Just as human as I am.

"What's wrong?" he asks softly.

"Nothing." I shake off the weird realization. Of course Arthur is human. He's just never been particularly important to me and wouldn't be now if he hadn't felt sorry for me and offered me this job.

"Well, something is wrong. You don't have to tell me, but don't lie to me."

Once again, that surge of annoyance rises inside me. The one that's not typical of me at all. I stick out my chin. "I can lie to you if I want."

"Sure you can. But why would you?"

"Who said I was?"

"I said you were. You might not talk a lot, but your face is expressive. I can read what you're feeling."

I suck in a sharp gasp. "You cannot!"

He arches his eyebrows. The silently skeptical response is more aggravating than any words would have been.

"I'm sure you think you can, but my thoughts and feelings aren't reduced to simple expressions. Whatever you see on my face is only part of what's there."

"You think I don't know that?"

"Well, I don't know. You were just now acting all smug and omnipotent about reading my expressions."

"Only because you doubted my ability to spot a lie. I'm like you. I don't care to be the center of attention, but that leaves me a lot of time to observe. I see a lot more than people think."

"I'm sure you do. You just don't care about it."

A frown causes his forehead to crease into three little lines. "What is that supposed to mean?"

"It means you've spent your whole life studying the world without ever actually engaging with it." I'm genuinely surprised that he took offense at my comment. "That's hardly new information, is it?"

"How would you know how much I engage with the world?"

"I'm sure I don't know everything, but I know the basics. You've never been married. You've never had kids. You don't seem to have a lot of friends. You travel some-times, but it's almost always alone. You don't even really have a job."

He's about to object. I see it on his face.

So I hurry on. "I know you work. Managing the family money and businesses and whatever. But you don't go into a workplace regularly or have daily interac-tion with other people. You watch the world from your safe, skeptical distance and assume that makes you superior."

His eyes narrow. For the first time in all the years I've known him, he looks genuinely angry. Not hot and fiery. But cold and hard as steel. "I've never believed myself superior."

I breathe out a soft, dubious laugh.

"You're hardly one to judge someone else for hiding from the world," he says, calm and dry and slightly bitter.

My spine stiffens. My jaw tightens. "My dad just died. I'm still grieving!"

"I know that. I wasn't talking about this past month, although anyone with common sense would tell you that numbing yourself from the pain isn't the way to get rid of it."

I gasp indignantly, but he goes on before I can argue.

"I mean your whole life. You put on this act that's molded around what you perceive other people want so no one hurts or rejects you. You shape yourself into an image no one can possibly object to, but it's also inevitably an image no one can know and no one can want."

I'm suddenly so angry my vision blurs briefly. I can't remember ever feeling such rage in my life. "Fuck you, Arthur Worthing."

"What a supremely lucid rejoinder."

My hands are actually shaking. I tighten them into fists. I swear I could launch myself at him and claw lines down his cool, arrogant face.

I don't. Of course I don't. I stand up. "If you don't think I'm right about you, then take a look at what you just did. You didn't like that I had any sort of insight into who you are, so you threw up walls and shaped your intelligence into a weapon. You said what you knew would make me angry, and you did it on purpose to get me to back off. You're not even willing to engage in a real conversation. Are you really surprised that I might assume you've never engaged in life?"

I can't believe I said that. I'm never so openly raw and emotional. Certainly not with a man as unknowable as Arthur.

Afraid I made a fool of myself and still shaking with anger, I stride out of the room.

Arthur doesn't stop me. For no good reason and completely irrationally, that fact is the most upsetting of all.

I go to my room. It's my only private space in this entire estate. It's a beautiful, luxurious suite. It's decorated exactly to my taste in a mix of pretty antiques, soft fabrics, a rose-and-taupe palette, and contemporary conveniences like remote-powered blinds and multiple spray functions in the large shower.

If I were on vacation, I couldn't have asked for more, but I've been too sad and distracted to enjoy it this month. I flop down onto the bed, staring up at the ornate molding on the ceiling and scowling as I picture Arthur's face.

It feels like I revealed too much. That's something I never do. It makes me feel naked. Vulnerable. Like Arthur now knows and sees far deeper into my soul than he has any right.

And he didn't even do it in a genuine attempt to get to know me. He did it to be mean. To push me away.

It doesn't matter that he was right. That I've done exactly what he said I do for as long as I remember—the way I've learned to get through life with no one but an unstable father to rely on.

The one time I had a chance to be myself, to shape a life around what I want and who I am rather than what I assume other people want, I let my father drag me away from it. Maybe I'm not capable of being different. Maybe I have no right to be angry with Arthur for pointing out that reality.

Maybe now he'll be so annoyed with me that he makes me leave.

Despite the fact that I first met him years ago, I really know very little about Arthur. Maybe he's the kind of man who would fire me for displeasing him.

I might have ruined even the temporary safety I have here in one foolish conversation.

With that in mind, I jump up from the bed and run back down the hall and downstairs. I find Arthur where I left him in the library.

He's just sitting there, staring at the empty desk chair I vacated. He blinks in surprise when he sees I've come back.

"I'm sorry," I say, composing my tone to sound apologetic and just slightly wry. "I'm not sure what got into me. I shouldn't have gotten upset and said all that."

He stands up, tilting his head slightly to peer at my face. "What?"

"I said I'm sorry."

"I heard what you said. But I don't understand what's going on here."

Baffled and slightly annoyed by his response to my generous apology, I have to fight not to frown at him. "I'm apologizing. What don't you understand?"

"I don't understand why. If anyone was at fault here, it's me. So why would you—?" He breaks off his question, realization twisting briefly on his face. "Damn it, Scarlett. Don't you dare."

"Don't I dare *what*?" I'm still trying to hold on to my pacifying smile, but it's hard. The man has to be the most confusing, frustrating person I've ever known.

"Don't you dare try to mollify me."

I suck in an indignant breath. "I'm not trying to mollify you!" My outrage feels righteous, but even as I say the words, I'm aware that they're not true. Of course I'm trying to mollify him. That's exactly what I came back down here to do.

"Yes, you are. You were real before, and now you're not. You're not sorry. You're still exasperated with me."

"I am not—"

"Stop lying to me." His voice isn't loud. I've never once heard him raise his voice. But it's commanding, authoritative.

Part of me wants to shrink, but I'm not going to give him the satisfaction. "What the hell do you want from me? I know my being here is an act of generosity on your part, and I don't want to act unappreciative. I'm sorry we argued. It's the last thing I want. I'll try—"

"Damn it, Scarlett," he says again, this time in a guttural mutter. "Do you actually think I'll fire you? Send you away? Just because you speak your mind?"

"Not for speaking my mind. For offending you."

"You didn't offend me. And what the hell kind of man do you take me for? You really think I'm the kind of person who would throw you out for something so petty?"

I stare up at him, anxious and jittery and utterly bewildered. The truth is that's exactly what I was afraid of, but evidently he finds the assumption deeply insulting.

"You did think that. You came back down to mend fences so I wouldn't send you away. Damn it all to hell. You really thought that about me?"

I open my mouth. Close it again. Swallow hard. Admit, "I didn't know."

"You should have known. You should know I'm not—"

"Why should I know?" I burst out. "It's not like I really know you."

"Of course you know—"

"I've known of you for a long time, but I've never known you well. You were my dad's friend. Not mine. And we both know my dad had no particular hang-ups over morality, either in himself or in other people. Why would I know the kind of man you are?"

That throws him off guard. He blinks and glances away, visibly thinking through what I said.

"Some men are driven by ego. Some men hold a grudge. And others don't want to waste their time with people who don't make them feel good about themselves. You could have been one of those. In any of those cases, you would have wanted me gone. I... I don't have anywhere else to go, and I don't have any resources. I've got to be careful."

"I see." His expression is finally softening. "I understand. So hear me now. No matter what you say to me, I'm never going to throw you out. You can stay here as long as you want. As long as you need to. Even after the library is cataloged. If you feel like you need to work, I can find another job for you to do. I don't want fear of being kicked out to be a factor in how you act toward me. I don't like to be mollified, and I've never been charmed in my life."

I'm relieved. No question. Maybe that explains why I giggle. "That I can believe."

"I'm sure. So take that worry off the table. You can say what you want."

"Thank you. For being clear on that. It... helps. It makes me feel better. Safer." I clear my throat as I sit down in the second side chair near the desk. "But I am sorry about being snippy."

"You're the least snippy person I've ever met." He sits

down too, his mouth softened like he's tempted to smile. "But I'd rather you be snippy than be..."

"Be what?"

"Empty. Fake. I'm sure a lot of men fall for it and see nothing but your big eyes and soft lips, but I can recognize the emptiness, and it bothers me. I'd much rather you be yourself even if you're in a bad mood."

His matter-of-fact assessment of my eyes and lips makes my cheeks warm, but there's a different kind of flutter in my chest prompted by the core of what he's saying. "Okay. As long as you'll... you'll do me the same courtesy and be real instead of always cool and smart."

"So you think I'm not really smart?"

It takes me a few seconds to realize that he's actually teasing. There's the slightest glint in his eyes. "Of course you're smart. I've never known anyone smarter. But you're more than that, and you don't like to act that way. If you can demand it of me, then I can demand it of you."

"Fair enough." He leans back in his chair, his shoulders relaxing and his mouth twitching up just slightly. "I guess we're more alike than we realized. Who would have thought?"

"I don't think we're that much alike."

"Not on the surface. But I think we've both learned not to trust other people, so we hide who we really are."

"I'm not that untrusting."

"Aren't you? Your first assumption was that I was an

asshole, and I hope I've never given you any reason to assume that about me."

"No. You've always been good to me. And my dad. But I..." With a shrug, I admit the truth, to myself as much as him. "I guess I don't really trust most people. Not in the way that matters. Not so I can really be myself with them."

"Your dad had a lot of good points, and I cared about him. But he did a real number on you. When I think about that, I deeply want to punch him."

I exhale a soft huff. "Yeah. I feel that way a lot too. With my dad, it's hard. Because there's so much about him to love and so much about him to hate. He did make it hard for me to trust people and to feel like life can be... stable. Solid. But it's not all my dad's fault. Part of it is just me." I pause briefly, then hear myself asking, "What made you the way you are?"

Arthur looks at me a long time. A piece of hair is hanging into his face, brushing lightly against his cheekbone. I really want to smooth it back. "A lot of things."

That's a nonanswer, but we aren't friends. He has no reason to share the most intimate parts of his life with me.

"So how is the work going?" he asks in a different tone. It's an obvious attempt to change the subject, but I'm relieved by it. "Are you making good progress?"

I start summarizing what I've been working on, but he asks too many questions, so I end up rambling on and on. I show him the updates in my cataloging system, and then we start looking at some of the rarer volumes. Before I know it, two hours have passed.

Stella comes in with a tray of hot chocolate and gingerbread cookies, smiling maternally as we chat on. She leaves without interrupting our conversation, although we both pause to thank her.

Our mugs are nearly empty and the cookies almost gone before I finally drop my eyes, wondering what got into me for babbling on this way.

I'm not a babbler. Anyone who knows me would agree.

But the past couple of hours have been the most enjoyable ones I've spent for the past year, ever since my father was arrested.

"Sorry for talking on and on," I say, the reflex to apologize so ingrained in me I say the words even knowing Arthur won't like them.

He narrows his eyes.

"Sorr—" I choke on the word.

"Were you about to apologize for apologizing?" Despite his wry tone, his eyes are warmer than I've ever seen them. Like melting chocolate.

"Of course not." I flash him a smile. "I'll try to do better. But seriously, I'm sure you have work to do."

"There's always work to do. This was a much better way to spend the afternoon."

I look up at him through my eyelashes, feeling shy

even as I smile. "It's not often I talk to someone who knows so much about books."

"Same." He glances into his mug and must see one remaining sip. He tilts it up to finish it.

When he swallows and lowers the mug, he has a sheen of liquid above his upper lip.

I don't understand the impulse. And I don't understand why I act on it. I'm not someone who is forward about physical touch, even with the men I used to date when I had some sort of social life. But for whatever reason, I'm compelled to reach over and swipe my thumb along the line of his lip, wiping away the residue of hot chocolate.

His skin is deliciously rough under the pad of my thumb. The friction makes me shiver. He grows very still, his eyes devouring my face.

I freeze with my hand still extended toward his lips.

He's not a man I'm supposed to be close to. Definitely not a man I'm supposed to touch.

But right now—in this moment—it's the only thing I want.

4

_____

I WAKE UP BREATHLESS. HOT. SHIFTING RESTLESSLY BENEATH my covers. And consumed by sensations of closeness, intimacy. The feel of Arthur's stubble beneath my thumb.

It's so real. Realer than anything I've experienced since I woke up in the hospital.

But it has to be a dream.

Right?

It couldn't be a lost memory. I never would have touched Arthur that way. I never would have wanted to.

It was a dream.

I sit up in bed, still sucking down air in thick rasps. My skin doesn't only feel hot. It feels tight. Too small for everything inside me. Stretched thin by a fullness, an intensity evoked by the idea of being with Arthur like that.

Compelled by an urge I don't understand, I jump out of bed, sliding on my slippers and hurrying toward my bedroom door. It's only been a couple of hours since I left Arthur in the library after finishing the hot chocolate we made. Now the clear memory of that scene is mingling with my dream. The lines are getting blurred. I have no idea what's real and what's not.

I need to know. Right now.

I head down the hall four doors until I reach Arthur's bedroom. I don't know why I know which room is his, but I do. I pound on the door.

"What?" The voice from inside is muffled at first, then clearer. "Come in. What's wrong?"

I've started opening the door when it swings away from me. He opened it himself and is now standing in the doorway, staring at me urgently.

He must not sleep in the undershirt he was wearing earlier. Right now he's got on nothing but the pajama pants. There's hair on his chest. A strong, graceful line to his shoulders and biceps. He's not totally flat or hard as a rock in the middle, but the slight softness near his waistline is more appealing to me than a perfect bodybuilder's form would have been.

His physicality briefly distracts me. I forget why I'm here.

"Scarlett? What the hell is wrong? Talk to me." He reaches out to take one of my shoulders, holding it in a firm grip.

"N-nothing. Sorry. I shouldn't have woken you up. But I was... I don't know. It was a dream. It felt so real, but I'm sure it was a dream."

I don't even remember any of the details anymore. Nothing except that sense of closeness with Arthur. His mouth. Warmth. Sweetness.

"What? What did you remember?" His fingers tighten in a quick squeeze.

"Nothing. I'm sorry." I blink a few times, trying to clear my mind. The dark fog has set in again, swirling in front of images and feelings I momentarily had a grasp on. Nothing is left but the lingering effect on my body.

I'm too hot again. Restless and kind of achy. I lower my eyes. "I'm sorry. I was dreaming. It was vivid, and it upset me. But I think it was just a dream now that I'm awake enough to think it through."

He's gotten control of his urgency now. He drops his hand and takes a step back, saying mildly, "Why don't you tell me what you dreamed, and maybe I can tell you if it was real or not."

"I... I can't even remember details anymore. I had them when I first woke up, but now they're gone. I'm sure we were in the library?"

"You and me?" It sounds almost like he's holding his breath.

"Yes. You were... You were there. We were... I don't know... talking. Maybe arguing. Then I... I..." I touched him.

"What did you do?" It's hard to tell because the room and hallway are so dark, but it looks like he might be as flushed as I am.

I touched him. I'm sure of it. Something about his mouth right now is evoking those same waves of feelings that were hitting me as I woke up earlier. But I'm convinced now it was a dream.

And I was about to admit it to him. I was dreaming of touching him. Dreaming of being close to him. Dreaming of his mouth.

I redden even more at the idea of admitting such an inappropriate truth to Arthur Worthing.

"It's all scattered. It was a dream. I don't know why I took it so seriously and came to wake you up. I'm sorry."

"You don't have to be sorry. You can wake me up anytime."

We stare at each other, both of us breathing heavily.

"Okay. Thanks. I'm... I'm..." I'm about to say I'm sorry again, but I've already said it more than once and he's dismissed it. "I think my mental processes are probably kind of screwed up by everything."

"They're not screwed up. You just can't remember everything. Give it some more time."

I nod, comforted by his calm assurance. Hopefully he's right.

I'm suddenly aware of his shirtlessness. His warm body only a few inches away. His hair is in wild disarray still. I want to run my fingers through it.

Desperately.

I shift from foot to foot. "Well."

"Well." He takes another step back. "You should go back to bed."

"I'm not tired."

"You should go anyway." His voice is gruffer than ever, but it's not angry. It's urgent in a different way.

I wish I could see his expression more clearly, but he's moved farther into the shadows.

Whatever the reason, he wants me to leave. I woke him up in the middle of the night for no real purpose.

"Okay. Yeah. I'll see you tomorrow."

"We can talk then. Good night, Scarlett."

"Good night."

I close the door as I step into the hallway. He swings the bedroom door closed before I can think of anything else to say.

Well.

That's that.

Maybe I'll remember something real eventually.

Maybe I'll understand what's always simmering beneath the surface of Arthur's composure.

Maybe one day I'll rediscover everything I've lost.

I want it now more than ever.

Several days later, I walk out of a commercial office building in Alexandria and look around until I spot the dark blue SUV. Arthur dropped me off at the front an hour ago, and he must have been waiting in view of the entrance because he's already driving over to pick me up.

I smile when I see his scarred, attractive face—so full of lines and rough edges and character—and his rumpled hair. His sober, watchful brown eyes.

I'm not sure why, but I really like the sight of him right now.

He smiles back, warm but slightly surprised. He leans over to push open the passenger door before I can reach the handle. "How did it go?" he asks as I climb in.

"Pretty good, I think. I like her, and she didn't make it weird even though it's strange I was seeing her as a counselor for months but can't remember any of it."

A few days ago, Arthur mentioned that I'd been seeing Dr. Esther Walters as a counselor and asked if I wanted to keep the appointments I'd made. I was hesitant but said yes because it seemed like the smart, mature thing to do.

My mind is such a mess right now that counseling definitely makes sense. I don't want to be foolish or petty or childish, resisting the things that might help me. But I'm also not in the habit of spilling out my most private thoughts and feelings to a stranger.

I was dreading the appointment, but Dr. Walters is quiet and gracious and didn't push as much as I feared. Talking through my strange situation wasn't as difficult as I imagined.

"You always liked her a lot." He hasn't started driving yet. He's still stopped by the curb as I settle myself and put on my seat belt.

"And the appointments seemed to... help me?"

"Yes. I think so. It took a while, but you started seeing progress. You worked through a lot of the emotional baggage from your father—at least, that's what you told me. And you seemed more... at peace. Settled." He's not looking at me now. He's staring out the windshield at an empty spot in the air. His voice thickens with a nameless poignance as he adds, "You were... happy."

"I was?"

He meets my eyes but then quickly looks away. "I think so." His breath catches. "I thought so."

I fight the urge to squirm, unsure why the soft words make me feel so vulnerable. "Oh. Okay. Well, I'll keep seeing her. It's been a long time since I remember being happy. I'd like to get there again."

Without thinking, I pull down the visor and study my reflection in the mirror. It's still the Scarlett I'm used to seeing—amber eyes, straight brown hair, fair skin that flushes easily. But I suddenly realize the face has, in fact, changed from what I remember before my dad died. I lost too much weight in those months in exile. My cheeks had hollowed out in a way that overemphasized my cheekbones, and the line of my jaw and neck had looked almost gaunt.

My appearance had been closer to a fashion-model ideal, but it wasn't who I am. I must have been eating better in the past few months. My face is fuller. Softer. Has more natural color.

I'm startled by how pretty I look right now in the afternoon light.

"What is it?" Arthur asks, noticing my distraction.

I shrug and flip up the mirror again. "I just realized I look better now than I did before my dad died. It makes me think you're right. I *was* doing better. I was happy."

"You'll get there again."

"I hope so." With a sigh, I shake away the wistful reflections. "She said I have another appointment on Friday. So I was seeing her twice a week?"

"You started at three times a week but then moved it to two when you were making progress."

"Oh. Okay. To tell you the truth, I'm surprised I even

thought of getting counseling." I slant him a look, wondering if he'll confirm my suspicions.

He does. "It was my idea. I suggested it. You were rather annoyed with me at first."

"Why was I annoyed? It seems like a reasonable suggestion given everything I was going through."

"It wasn't because you thought it was unreasonable. It was because you thought I was intruding on your life. You didn't appreciate that."

I can't help but giggle. "That seems more like me. How did you convince me to go?"

"I didn't. You thought about it and came back to me and said you were sorry for being snippy and that counseling might be worth trying. You did some research and liked what you read about Dr. Walters, so you made an appointment."

"Huh. That was very mature and sensible of me. Good for me."

He chuckles now, warm and almost fond. "I thought so too."

"So I guess I'll keep the two appointments a week. Seems like I could use them." That brings back another question I've been wondering. "By the way, how did I get to my appointments?"

He's finally pulled away from the curb and turns onto a busy road. He frowns and shoots me a quick look. "What do you mean?"

"I mean how do I get to the appointments,. I don't have a car, and I'll need to get myself to my appointments from now on. Did I Uber or something?"

"No. I drove you."

My mouth drops open. "You drove me? All this way two or three times a week?"

"Yes."

"But... but why? It's not just the drive. It's waiting an hour while I'm in there. Why did I let you?"

"You offered to get yourself to your appointments another way, but driving you is no trouble. I like getting out sometimes, and I don't waste the hour doing nothing. I make calls and return emails. The arrangement worked fine for both of us."

I'm still gaping at him, but he's shrugged the issue off like it's nothing.

It doesn't feel like nothing to me. He took nearly three hours out of his afternoons two or three times a week. I simply can't understand how I allowed it.

"If you don't want me to drive you," he says more quietly, almost subdued, "we can figure out something else."

"Oh. Yeah. I don't know. Maybe we can just play it by ear?" It feels like I somehow hurt his feelings, but I don't understand why or how.

"That would be fine." He clears his throat and gives his

head a little shake like he wants to brush off the awkward topic the way I do. "Do you feel like a treat?"

"A treat?"

"A food-related treat?"

"Oh." I blink, surprised but also rather excited. "I'm always up for a food-related treat."

"Ice cream sound okay?"

"Ice cream sounds great."

"Okay. Good." He checks his blind spot before merging over into the next lane. After a minute, he moves into the far-left lane and then pulls into a turn lane at a light.

I'm quiet as he's maneuvering through traffic, but when he's waiting for the light to change, I ask, "By the way, they said I didn't owe anything in Dr. Walters's office when I asked."

"You don't. Your insurance covers counseling."

"What insurance? Oh my goodness, I just realized all my hospital bills. Even with insurance, I probably owe—"

"It's all taken care of," he says, a bit stiffer than before.

"How is it taken care of?"

"When you started working for me, I got you a health insurance plan. It's a good one, so it covers a lot. Anything it doesn't comes to me, and I take care of it."

"But—"

"But nothing. You work for me. It's my responsibility to make sure you're covered."

"But not in everything! No employer does that. And I

saw I had a new banking app on my phone, so I checked it and there's way too much money in there for six months' work. Did I get money some other way?"

He shakes his head. "Your dad's assets were all frozen, and then you worked with the authorities to arrange for what he had to go toward reimbursing his victims. You're free and clear legally, in case you were wondering. You cooperated with the FBI and the US attorney on your dad's case, and they aren't charging you with anything. But there's no money left from your father."

"I didn't think there would be. But then what's the money in my bank account?"

"That's your salary from your job."

"But it's too much! Especially since you give me room and board and pay all my medical expenses and who knows what else."

His shoulders are stiffer than ever. He's not meeting my eyes. "You've brought your expertise to a difficult and time-consuming project. It's not too much."

Part of me still wants to argue, but he's not entirely wrong. Skills and knowledge like mine are often undervalued, but I worked hard to gain them. And cataloging that library can't possibly have been an easy job.

Plus whatever amount he's paid me is a drop in the ocean of the Worthing fortune.

Finally I say softly, "Thank you. Not just for the compensation but for everything you've done for me. I'm not sure..." My voice breaks. "I'm not sure what would have happened to me if it hadn't been for you. I'm so completely alone."

Our eyes meet for a moment before he breaks the gaze.

"You aren't alone. If I weren't here, Jenna would have helped you. With your experience, you could have gotten another job."

"Maybe. But still. Thank you."

He swallows. Doesn't look back at me. "You're welcome."

He takes me to an old-fashioned ice-cream parlor that delights me. I try not to act like a child, but I'm beaming as I gaze around at the retro decor and study the dozens of unique flavors in the big ice-cream cartons beneath the plexiglass.

The young woman behind the counter grins when we reach the front of the line. "You're back! I wondered where you two went."

I blink in surprise. Evidently we're regulars here.

"Our schedule got thrown out of whack for a couple of weeks," Arthur says casually. Then he turns to me. "What would you like?"

"I don't know. I can't choose."

"You can get the Kit and Kaboodle," the woman suggests. "That has some of everything. You can share it."

I have no idea what that is, but it's better than being put on the spot for a decision. So I nod and smile, and she looks excited as she puts together the biggest ice-cream concoction I've ever seen in my life.

"Oh my God!" I breathe as the scoops and toppings pile up in a large bowl. "What have I done?"

The woman behind the counter laughs, and Arthur is smiling, his eyes resting on my face.

After he pays, Arthur carries the ice-cream monstrosity over to a small table with two chairs near the window.

I can't stop giggling as he sets the bowl in the middle of the table and we both make relatively small inroads from each side. It's delicious but also ridiculously too much.

Arthur is clearly enjoying it too. Not just the ice cream but the experience. His shoulders are shaking with amusement. His expression is relaxed, almost soft. He chuckles when I playfully spoon-fight with him for the small mound of quadruple chocolate.

We don't talk much, but we don't have to.

I have a really good time. And I'm absolutely convinced that he has a good time too.

Coming home feels like the end of a date.

No matter how much I try to talk myself out it, I simply can't shake the feeling.

On the ride home, Arthur plays music from his phone through the car speakers. It's a collection of my favorite singer/songwriter. From what I've picked up, his tastes in music are somewhat eclectic, but I have to assume he knows she's my favorite and added the music to his phone just for me.

I have a good time with the music, and every time I check his expression, he's relaxed and smiling, so he can't mind the selection too much. When the best song plays, I start singing with it automatically, and I've gotten to the second verse before I realize what I'm doing. I stop abruptly in case Arthur finds my singing annoying or silly.

He slants me a frown and picks up singing the chorus in a pleasant but unexceptional baritone.

He knows all the words. I gape at him, trying not to giggle.

"Is something wrong?" he asks, exaggeratedly lofty.

"How do you know this song?"

"I've heard it enough." He doesn't explain, but I wonder if it's because he's played it that much for me. "It's cleverly written."

The mild words from a man like him are high praise. I feel like preening. He reaches over to restart the song, and we sing it together. He knows the next song on the playlist too. I can't seem to stop smiling as we sing.

We're home before I want the drive to be over, and as we come into the house, I feel that same excited, breathless, slightly insecure feeling you get at the end of a date. We look at each other, standing in the entry hall.

I really want to kiss him, and I have to lower my eyes to hide it, occasionally peeking up through my lashes to see what he's doing.

He's not doing anything. Just standing there, gazing down at me, his hair windblown despite being pulled back at his neck and one side of his collar askew.

His eyes are so soft. I never imagined he'd look at me that way.

I never imagined *anyone* would look at me that way.

I have no idea what might happen, but then Stella walks through the back hallway and pauses when she sees us to ask how our outing was.

Disappointed and relieved both by the interruption, I tell her the appointment was good and we stopped for ice cream afterward. I tell Arthur I'm going to take a walk since I clearly need some space and fresh air, and he heads back to his home office to work.

I wander around the gardens and grounds, giving myself a sensible lecture about how I'm not in fit mental condition right now to make good decisions about relationships and that Arthur might feel sorry for me but doesn't likely think about me as anything other than his friend's daughter and maybe a foolish little girl with a crush.

It's a depressing sequence of thoughts but effectively puts a damper on my rising giddy thrills.

Eventually I make my way back to the old stables. Previous generations of Worthings kept horses, but not in my lifetime. The stables were solidly constructed and are still standing. I'm about to pass by them when I notice a flicker of motion at the entrance.

Curious, I glance inside and see a long tail before it disappears into one of the stalls.

I'm sure it's a dog. As far as I know, there are no animals on this estate other than scattered wildlife. I tread carefully over the muddy ground and peek into the stall.

It is a dog. A gaunt, unkempt mixed breed—maybe part border collie—with a dirty face and matted fur. It's trying to hide behind an old crate. Its tail swishes above the top edge when I say, "Hey, buddy. What are you doing back there? Are you okay?"

The dog doesn't come out, so I crouch down lower and keep talking. "Come on out, buddy. I'm not going to hurt you. You shouldn't be out here by yourself. Someone should be taking care of you. Come on, fella."

He repositions and sticks his head around the corner of the crate to look.

I smile. "Hey, buddy. There you are. I bet you're a real

good boy. You wanna come out and say hi to me?" I extend one hand.

He slowly steps over and sniffs at my hand a long time. I wish I had some food, but he responds to my gentleness anyway. Comes a little closer until I can cautiously stroke his head. Scratch his ears.

He gives a little whimper and nuzzles me.

Ridiculously, I'm near tears at the dog's pathetic gratitude for basic human kindness. I talk to him and pet him for a long time. Then I decide he needs something to eat and some water, so I get up to leave.

He darts behind the crate as soon as I start to exit the stables.

I have to sneak into the kitchen to get some leftover chicken and rice, a bottle of water, and a metal bowl.

As soon as the dog spies me returning to the stable, he comes to greet me, wagging his long tail.

He scarfs down the food and laps at the water. I hang out with him for almost an hour until I realize it will be dinner soon and Arthur will be wondering where I am.

Arthur seems to notice I've been up to something. He asks what I've been doing, then asks if anything is wrong. I tell him everything is fine but don't tell him about the dog.

For the next two days, I visit the stable at least three times a day, bringing food and water and doing my best to comb out the dog's matted fur. We're best friends by the second day.

On Friday, I ask Arthur if we can stop by a drugstore on the way back from the counseling appointment, explaining I need some personal items. He doesn't question the request. I'm carrying an oversized purse that can conceal the small bag of dog food I buy. I also buy a box of tampons I carry out in a plastic store bag so Arthur will see the personal items that were my excuse for the stop.

Having the dog food makes it easier. The dog eats it just as happily as the deli meat and leftovers I've been sneaking out of the kitchen.

Arthur keeps asking if everything is okay, and I keep telling him nothing.

The dog feels like mine now. I don't want to turn him over to an animal shelter.

On Saturday after lunch, Arthur seems to be lingering, so I tell him I'm going to take a walk.

"You want some company?" he asks, eyeing me with a discreet kind of scrutiny.

"No, I'm good." I give him my best smile. "I'm sure you have better things to do."

"It's Saturday. I don't really have to work."

"But you don't have to hang out with me." When it looks like he's going to object, I hurry on. "I like taking walks alone. I'm good."

He frowns and opens his mouth to launch into more questioning, but I don't give him the chance. I stop in the bathroom to give Arthur time to give up and move on, and then I walk outside by a side door and head for the stables.

It rained this morning, so the ground is muddier than normal. I have to test every step to make sure I don't slip in the mud puddles at the entrance of the stables.

The dog gives a happy yip when he sees me approach and runs over for hugs and pets.

He's dirtier than ever despite my attempts to get him clean. He really needs a good bath.

Eventually I'm going to have to do something. Tell Arthur. Ask if there's any way I can keep him.

The Worthings never had any pets, not even in the historic portraits in the third-floor gallery. Nothing but horses, and those were mostly an investment and for recreation. Not for emotional bonding.

Arthur isn't going to want to bring a stray dog into his beautiful house.

"What are we going to do?" I ask with a smile, sitting on a crate and scratching behind the dog's ears. "If I have to, I guess I can try to find my own place and then I can adopt you. You'd like that, wouldn't you?"

The dog's brown eyes are excited and adoring, gazing up at me unwaveringly. His tail is wagging slowly.

"I don't really want to leave. I kind of like it here. But I will if I have to."

The dog appears to be listening, cocking his head like he's trying to understand what I'm saying. But suddenly he whirls around and growls low in his throat, pointed toward the entrance of the stables.

I stand up, startled and worried.

The dog suddenly lunges. There's some sort of scuffle, so quick I have no idea what's happening. I hear growling and muttered cursing and gasps. By the time I come around the corner to look, the dog is poised victoriously over his captive.

Arthur.

Flat on his back in the mud.

Shocked and breathless, I call the dog off and lean over to check on Arthur.

He's glaring up at me with narrowed eyes. "What the hell, Scarlett?"

"Did he hurt you?"

"No, he didn't hurt me. He just knocked me over in the fucking mud and wouldn't let me up. What the hell is even happening here?"

"I'm sorry. He must have thought you were a threat. He didn't bite you?"

"No, he didn't bite me." Arthur lifts his head and gives the dog a cold glare. "What is he doing here?"

"I don't know. He's a stray who somehow ended up here. What are *you* doing here?"

"You've been up to something and wouldn't tell me what it was. So I came to find out what was going on with you." He hefts himself to a sitting position, shooting the dog a wary glare. The back of his hair and shirt and pants are coated with mud.

"You followed me?" Maybe that's an irrelevant detail, but I fixate on it. "Why would you do that?"

"I wouldn't have if you'd told me what you were up to. I was worried."

"That doesn't mean you can spy on me. Seriously, Arthur, you can't—" I break off because the dog, evidently picking up the indignation in my tone, starts growling at Arthur again. "It's fine, fella. He's not going to hurt me." I extend a hand, and the dog runs over to be petted.

Arthur stands up, wincing as he straightens.

"Did you hurt yourself?" I ask, distracted from my annoyance by concern that the fall actually injured him.

"No." He's muttering but doesn't look genuinely angry. Mostly just grumpy. "I'm simply too old to be knocked to the ground by a militant canine."

"He's not militant. He hasn't been aggressive at all, and he didn't bite you. He was trying to protect me because you were sneaking around."

Arthur makes a face and an ineffective attempt to wipe some of the mud off the rear of his pants.

Something about the combination of his grumpiness and the mess of his clothes, so incongruous to his typical cultured sophistication, hits me just then. I choke on a giggle.

He narrows his eyes even more. He's smug and annoyed and covered with mud.

It's hopeless then. I burst into helpless laughter.

"Seriously?" he asks dryly.

"I'm sorry. I really am."

The dog wags his tail excitedly and evidently decides this means Arthur isn't an enemy. He walks over to nose one of Arthur's hands.

I see Arthur give the dog a quick pet before he grumbles, "Now you try to make up to me? After you knock me over in the mud?"

"He didn't mean to."

"I think that's exactly what he meant to do." Arthur sighs and shakes his head. "Well, come on. I need to get cleaned up, and this dog needs it even more than me."

"So he can come inside?"

"I have no doubt I'm going to regret it, but yes, he can come inside."

5

PRESENT

BRINGING THE DOG INTO THE HOUSE IS QUITE A PRODUCTION.

He's a good-natured, agreeable animal, but he's also incredibly excited about the attention and the new surroundings. He spins and pants and investigates every crack and corner with eager sniffs. At one point he springs off down the hall and barrels through the dining room until he reaches the kitchen.

Stella greets the newcomer with a repertoire of "Oh my!"s varying from shocked to bewildered to amused. Billy appears from the yard, wanting to know the cause of all the commotion. He volunteers to give the dog a bath, and I go with him to one of the guest showers to help.

It's not an easy process. The dog clearly doesn't think getting hosed with the shower spray is treatment that's appropriate to his breed and dignity. He keeps trying to squirm his way out of the bath until both Billy and I are soaking wet.

When we finally rinse off the shampoo and make a gesture toward towel drying some of the moisture off, the dog has clearly had enough. He makes a frantic leap that moves him out of my and Billy's reach and then makes a dash for the door of the bathroom, which was left open just a crack.

Now free, he starts zooming up and down the hallway in gleeful sprints, leaving a path of scattered water droplets and a couple of toppled chairs in his wake.

Billy and I are nearly doubled over with laughter as we chase him. Arthur was in his room, showering and changing after his muddy adventure, but he comes to the door to see what's causing the uproar.

The dog seizes the opportunity to push past Arthur and run ecstatic circles around his bedroom. Then he jumps onto the bed and scratches up a nest in Arthur's thick, expensive, pristinely white duvet and flops down on the fluffy pile of bedding.

I'm still trying not to laugh, but I'm also a little worried about Arthur's reaction. He was already annoyed with being knocked into the mud. Now his lovely bed is all messed up by a wet dog.

He narrows his eyes in exaggerated disapproval. "You have got to be kidding me."

"I'm sorry," I gasp, crossing my arms over my stomach as if I might hold the amusement inside. "We tried to hold on to him, but he got away."

"I can see that. Is there a particular reason he chose my bed to ravage?"

"Well, probably because it was so nice and clean and comfy."

"It's not nice and clean anymore."

"No." I look at the floor because his aggrieved expression is making me giggle even more. "I guess not. Sorry about that."

He lets out a long breath. "Are you sorry?"

I dart a quick look at him and suddenly realize he just got out of the shower. His hair is wet, combed out and pulled back smoothly at the nape of his neck. Without the softness of his rumpled hair, he looks sleeker, harder. The chiseled lines of his face are more pronounced—high cheekbones, broad forehead, striking jaw. He's wearing a gray T-shirt—damp around the neckline—and a pair of darker gray sweatpants that are more worn than anything I've ever seen him in.

He's incredibly hot—familiar but also disturbingly sexy. Even his feet are bare, and the sight of them on the polished hardwood floor does something weird and intense to my insides.

"Scarlett?" he asks in a different tone, ducking his head slightly to better see my expression.

I shake away the unexpected attraction and reply to his earlier question. "I am sorry. The dog has caused you a lot of trouble, and I feel responsible for the dog."

His mouth twitches up. "You *are* responsible for the dog."

"Am I going to have to find him another home?"

"Don't you want to keep him?"

"Of course I want to keep him! But this is your house. And if you don't want him here, I'd have to—"

He gives his head a little shake. "What the hell do you take me for? You think I'd throw out a helpless dog?"

"Well... I mean... I know you wouldn't harm a dog, but this is just a stray. You might ask me to find him somewhere else to live. You're not an animal person."

"Why would you say that?" He sounds curious more than offended.

"I don't know. You've never had any pets."

"My dad wouldn't let us. I always liked animals."

"Then why didn't you get one on your own?"

He shrugs. "I didn't do a lot of things I could have done." He glances back at the dog, who has lowered his head and is snoring blissfully. "He's not a bad dog. He didn't try to bite me even when he thought I was a threat. He's smart, and he's clearly bonded with you. We might want to get him some training."

"Of course."

"I've called around to some local vets and shelters, and no one knows of a missing dog that matches his description, so it looks like he's a real stray. We'll have to take him to the vet soon to get examined, and he'll have to be put on heartworm prevention and flea control."

I raise a hand to cover my mouth. "So we can keep him?"

He looks at me for a little longer than I'd expect before he answers. "Yes. We can keep him. But he doesn't get to make a home in my bed."

With another giggle—as much relief as amusement—I reach over to nudge the dog off the bed. He gives an indignant huff and flops down on the area rug instead.

There's a big wet spot now in the middle of Arthur's duvet.

Before I can apologize, he pulls off the duvet and starts stripping the cover off.

I stare at him in surprise. Not that he'd want to change his bedding but that he'd do it himself instead of letting Stella do it.

"Stella is busy in the kitchen," Arthur says, clearly reading my mind. "No need to bother her when I can do it myself." He leans over to pull a clean duvet cover out of a leather storage bench under one of the windows.

"Oh. Of course. I just didn't..."

His lips tighten slightly. "You didn't what? Think I was capable of making a bed?"

"No. No, of course that's not it."

He waits for me to continue, but I have no idea what to say.

"You assumed I wouldn't let you keep a dog. You assumed I wouldn't make my own bed. What else have you been assuming about me that I should know?"

My cheeks flush hot. "I'm sorry. I just don't..." I clear my throat. "I know we got to know each other, but I don't remember it. So I'm left mostly with the impressions of you I had before I came here. But you're right. You've been nothing but thoughtful and generous with me, and I have no reason to expect you not to continue to be so."

He gives that slight nod of acknowledgment. "So you've been feeding the dog for days, I assume? Was it Tuesday you found him?"

"Yeah. In the afternoon. How did you know?"

"Because that's when you started acting secretive. I knew you were keeping something from me. You were distracted. And you'd disappear for hours. I couldn't figure out what the hell was going on, and you wouldn't tell me." His expression reflects the frustration he must have felt.

"What trouble could I have gotten into here? Did you think I was running off to meet a secret lover or something?"

There's a brief flicker on his face that makes me realize my flippant, teasing words might actually be true.

I gasp. "You thought that? Seriously? Where on earth would I have met a lover to be secret about?"

"I had no idea. But something was going on with you, and I needed to know what it was. I wasn't really spying on you. I hope you don't think your privacy was invaded too much. But I did follow you this afternoon so I could see what you were doing." He looks almost sheepish but not particularly sorry.

I don't have it in me to be angry with him at the moment. "Next time just ask."

"I did ask. You said you were taking a walk and wanted to be alone."

"Oh. Well. Yeah."

He's almost smiling now. "Yeah."

"I didn't think you'd want a dog."

"Why would you think I wouldn't do anything to make you happy?"

I gasp and shoot my eyes up to his face.

His mouth twists. He glances away like he didn't mean to say what he said. He adds, "I'm trying to be a decent guy."

"You *are* a decent guy." I reach over and squeeze his upper arm, liking how warm and firm and solid it feels beneath my grip. "Thank you."

"You're welcome." His face clears, relaxes. "Now maybe

you can find that wet dog a better place to sleep than my bedroom."

I giggle and call for the dog to follow me out, part of me wishing we both were allowed to stay.

An hour later, the dog and I have settled in on the big, cushy couch in the media room.

The dog is sound asleep, wound in a tight ball on a throw blanket I spread out so his wet fur wouldn't mess up the couch. I'm idly scanning my phone and slouched on the middle cushion, close enough so I can occasionally pet him, and I've got a second blanket spread over my lap and legs.

I'm perfectly comfortable, and even a sleeping dog is good company. But occasionally I wonder where Arthur is. What he's doing.

He said he didn't have to work on Saturday, but I guess he's still too busy to hang out with me.

The visual of him just out of the shower with wet hair and bare feet flickers through my mind occasionally. A bit too often for my comfort.

I spent so many years barely thinking about the man at all. He was just an older guy, someone my dad knew, a piece of background setting. But other than a month or two when I developed that ill-advised crush on him—in itself insignificant since I had a crush on almost everyone back then—he never lingered in my mind in any real way.

Now my heart speeds up whenever he's around. A warm anticipation lingers in my belly whenever there's a chance he might be passing by. I imagine scenarios where I could be closer to him. I mentally relive every interaction we have over and over again.

It's silly. Futile. Surely nothing more than an infatuation and prompted by the fact that I don't have anyone else in my life and the amnesia has twisted my normal perspectives. Arthur would probably be appalled if he found out the direction my thoughts have been drifting.

He's being nice, and I'm turning it into something more.

So I give myself yet another mental lecture and try to distract myself on my phone, texting Jenna for a while and then researching the best heartworm and flea preventions.

I must have effectively diverted my attention because I'm completely unprepared when Arthur strolls into the room and lowers himself to the couch cushion on the opposite end from the dog.

"Hey," I say, my heartbeat accelerating despite my best attempts at reasonable calm. "I thought you might be working."

He shrugs. "It's Saturday. Not much going on."

That's what he'd said earlier, but I still thought he might do some work. "Oh. That's good then."

"If you want to be alone, I can hang out elsewhere."

"No, I don't want to be alone." That sounds kind of needy, so I rephrase. "I mean, I'm happy for you to hang out with me."

I'm not sure my second try was much better.

His mouth twitches up in that appealing way he has. "That's good then. How's the dog doing?"

"He thinks he's landed in paradise. He can't believe his luck." I stroke the animal's damp head gently. "Thanks for taking him in. Taking *us* in."

He doesn't respond when I would have expected him to, so I glance over to check his face. He's staring at the blank television screen in front of us, his mouth working very slightly, like he's mentally composing a reply.

I wait for it, nearly holding my breath.

Finally he says in a low, rough murmur, "You assume taking you in is a burden on me. It's not."

On the surface, the words convey nothing significant, but my chest bursts into flutters anyway. "Okay." I swallow hard until my voice sounds more normal. "But thank you all the same. From both of us."

He inclines his head, still not meeting my eyes. Then he straightens up, his expression relaxing. "What are you going to name him?"

"I don't know. I've been thinking of possibilities, but nothing has hit me yet. You got any ideas?"

"Chaos? Disaster? Apocalypse?"

I giggle, giving him a playful little push. "I'm not going to give him a mean name. He needs a respectable name."

"Herman? Archibald? Winston?" His tone is bone dry and tickles me even more.

"Not that respectable. I was thinking more like William or Michael."

He chuckles. "That dog is neither a William nor a Michael. He's maybe a Fred."

"Fred?" My eyes widen. I turn to study the sleeping dog beside me. "I kind of like it."

"I was teasing."

"I know you were, but I still like it. I think he's a Fred."

"Only you would name your dog Fred." His voice is so amused and fond that the words feel like a compliment.

"To be perfectly accurate, you're the one who named him. So he's Fred. Fred Kingston-Worthing." I'm smiling as I play with one of the dog's ears. Then I realize I might have been too presumptuous. "He doesn't have to take your name too if you don't want. He can just be Fred Kingston."

Arthur is staring at the darkened TV screen again. "No, he can have my name."

"Okay then."

We sit in slightly awkward silence. I have no idea what he's thinking, and it's driving me crazy that I can't read his mind. Finally I say, "You want to watch something?" I nod toward the television.

He appears relieved at the distraction. "Sure. We can find a movie."

"Sounds good to me. Whatever you want. I'm good with anything."

He pulls up a streaming service and lands on a classic movie from the forties. I love old movies, so I happily agree.

Then I wonder if he already knew my movie preferences and chose one accordingly.

I don't ask. I pull the blanket up to get cozy and settle in to watch.

After about an hour, Stella comes in with a tray of fish tacos and salad for our dinner. Also a bottle of chardonnay. She's smiling covertly—like she has a secret—as she fills two glasses and arranges the plates for us. I notice her expression and wonder why she's in such a good mood.

Everything is delicious, and I even accept a second glass of wine although I haven't been drinking much these past two weeks because of the head injury. Fred wakes up to beg for fish tacos but then immediately goes back to sleep. When we finish the movie, we take Fred out to do his business but then return to the couch. Arthur queues up another movie without asking. It makes me happy because it means the evening isn't over yet.

The combination of the wine and food and comfortable surroundings get to me eventually. First my eyes start drifting shut. Then my head leans back and my body slides to the side so that I'm leaning against Arthur.

He adjusts in a way that feels a lot more comfortable. I'm too out of it to figure out how he moved or why I like it so much, but I feel warmer, safer. I snuggle in until details of my surroundings blur into contented darkness.

6

I'M EXHAUSTED BUT ODDLY EXHILARATED AS I CLIMB INTO Arthur's SUV after another appointment with Dr. Walters.

As always, he scans my face as I pull my seat belt on. "Good appointment?"

"Yeah. I think so. It was hard but good. It feels like I've had a few minor breakthroughs."

"Anything you'd like to share?"

After living and working with him for more than two months, I'm used to talking to Arthur now. I'm also convinced of the fact that his questions aren't idle or mere courtesy. He wants to know how I'm doing and what I'm thinking.

It matters to him.

So I explain to him what I talked through with Dr. Walters today—about how I've always let my father control me, believing I needed to do what he wanted in order to earn his love and how it's only now I'm realizing the problem was never the things I did but that I didn't understand what love is supposed to be.

Arthur listens, occasionally murmuring affirmation or asking a clarifying question. We stop by our favorite ice-cream parlor and get waffle cones, continuing our discussion.

When I've finally shared everything, we sit in thoughtful silence until I ask, "What about you?"

"What about you?"

"Did your parents screw you up too?"

He gives a dry huff. "Oh yes."

"Your mom died when you were pretty young, right?"

"Yeah. I was twelve. My dad was a hard man. Your father did love you—even if he got everything wrong about how he did it. I have no proof that my father loved me at all. My mom was softer. I think she did love me, but she was completely cowed by my father's authority, so she wasn't able to protect me much even while she was alive."

A chill runs down from my throat to the base of my spine. "Did he... Did he hurt you?"

"Physically, only once or twice. When he was drunk." He's staring out the window next to our small table.

"There are other ways to hurt a child."

"Yes," Arthur murmurs, rough texture in the brief words. "There are."

"I'm sorry. Is that why... Is that why you never had many friends?"

"I guess so. I think I learned to live alone, to not trust anyone to genuinely care about me. The other kids never really liked me when I was a boy, but they never picked on me. Because I'm a Worthing, I was off-limits for bullying. Mostly they just left me alone, and I thought that was simply who I am."

"Did you try to have relationships? When you grew up?"

"Sure. I made some friends. Like your father. I did try. And I dated. I went through phases when I dated a lot. But nothing ever... clicked." He sighs and closes his eyes. "I look back now and can understand why. You were right about me that night in the library last month. Every single word. I was always holding back, hiding who I really am so I would never be vulnerable. So I would never feel the way I did as a kid, desperately wanting my dad's love but never getting it."

I reach over and cover his hand, which is resting on the table. I don't know what to say, but I want him to know I hear him, that I understand.

Finally he turns his hand slightly, squeezes mine, and then releases it. "I can't blame it on my dad. He didn't do right by me, no question. But I'm a forty-six-year-old man. I've had plenty of time to work through all the baggage, and I never did."

"Why didn't you?"

He breaks off a piece of waffle cone and chews on it thoughtfully. "Never seemed worth the effort and pain."

"I think it would be."

He finally turns back to give me a little smile. "You think so?"

"Yeah. I think so."

Something thick and quivering lingers in the air between us as we gaze at each other. Then Arthur checks his watch and says we better head home.

When we arrive at the house, Stella asks what we feel like for dinner, and I tell her something light because we had ice cream earlier. "Maybe something easy to eat," I suggest, having an idea and jumping on it. "I was thinking about watching a movie or something later."

"That sounds like an excellent idea," Stella says, appearing pleased and encouraging. She glances over toward Arthur.

I wait too, swallowing over a follow-up question.

When I first arrived, we always ate dinner together, and he'd make a point of asking me questions and sustaining pleasant conversation. But in the past couple of weeks, he's been working through dinner a lot. And when he does eat with me, he's quiet and kind of aloof. The meals are awkward in a way they've never been before, and I don't understand why.

We get along so well on our trips to and from my counseling appointments and when he stops by the library to see how my work is going. Why has he suddenly gotten weird over dinner?

Maybe eating while we watch a movie would be more relaxed and natural. I want to spend time with him, and he's making it difficult.

He doesn't do anything with the prompt I left hanging. Simply inclines his head and mumbles he'll be in his office if anyone needs him.

I make a face at his retreating back and catch Stella shaking her head like she's half-amused and half-frustrated.

I know the feeling.

There's a nicely supplied workout room in the basement here, so I spend almost an hour lifting some weights and working out on the elliptical. Then I take a shower and change into soft pink lounge pants and a loose V-neck top. When it's dinnertime, I head downstairs, wondering if I'll be brave enough to ask Arthur to eat and watch a movie with me.

It's not like I'm going to make a move on him despite the direction my daydreams have started to drift. I want his company. Surely there isn't anything wrong with that.

I'm in the hall, walking past the door to Arthur's home office, when I hear muffled voices from inside.

Stella is in there, talking to him. She says, "I'm just saying she was giving you an obvious hint, and it went right over your head."

"She wasn't hinting. You're imagining things. If anything, she was trying to get out of eating dinner with me."

"She was not. She wanted you to say that sounded like fun and ask if you could join her. I am not the clueless one here."

I've never heard Stella sound so sharp, argumentative. I had no idea she was in the habit of talking to Arthur this way. I know I should keep walking. Eavesdropping is wrong. But I'm not sure how anyone in my situation could resist.

I certainly don't. I pause and keep listening.

"I'm not being clueless. I need to be careful. It would be easy for me to be inappropriate in these circumstances. I'm old enough to be her father—"

"You'd be an awfully young father. You're not even twenty years older than—"

"Even so, I'm much too old for her. She's young and beautiful and brilliant and so sweet. She'll eventually find a young, gifted man unburdened by baggage, one who can give her the life she deserves. If I'm always hanging around her, she'll start to get uncomfortable with me, and that's the last thing I want to happen."

"Are you sure that's the problem?"

"What does that mean?"

"Maybe you have other reasons for keeping your distance. Maybe you're feeling things you don't know what to do with and are trying to run away—"

"That is not it at all." His voice is cool and clipped. Most people would shrink back when faced with that particular tone from him.

Stella snorts. "You can keep telling yourself that, but age isn't always the obstacle you want to make it, and I have eyes in my head, you know. I've known you most of your life, and I've never seen you as happy as you've been since she arrived."

It sounds like Stella is about to leave, so I whirl around and return down the hall to the back stairs that I always take to come down from my room.

I'm flushed and flustered and oddly giddy as I try to compose a natural expression and make it look like I've only now come downstairs.

Stella is frowning as she closes Arthur's office door. When she sees me, she says, "Hello, dear. Dinner will be ready in about half an hour."

"Okay. That sounds good." I smile at her and think quickly. "Is he busy in there?"

"Not as busy as he wants to pretend."

I'm not sure what to do with that comment, so I ignore it, tapping on his office door.

"Come," he calls out gruffly.

"Hey," I say, as friendly and natural as I can conjure in these circumstances. "If you're busy, it's fine, but I wanted to see if you wanted to watch a movie with me."

He blinks at me from behind his desk like he just woke up from sleep.

"It's fine if you don't," I add. "But I'd kind of like the company."

I'm quite sure I never would have had the courage to offer such a direct invitation if I hadn't overheard his conversation with Stella. But I did hear it.

I suddenly have hope when I didn't before.

Arthur makes a guttural sound, turning his head to look at his computer screen and then shifting back to me. "Okay. Sure. Okay. If you're sure."

He almost never sounds so flustered. It makes me want to hug myself.

"I'm sure."

"Okay. Then sure. I don't have anything else I need to work on today."

"Great. I'm glad."

"Great."

I hear Stella chuckling softly as she makes her way down the hall.

We go to the media room and find an old movie to watch. I love black-and-white classics, the kind that star Humphrey Bogart or Katharine Hepburn or Cary Grant or even Fred Astaire. Arthur appears pleased with my taste in films, and we pick out one to watch as we sit on the couch together.

We chat occasionally, and Stella brings us Thai chicken wraps and a bottle of wine. I have a really good time, so much so that I suggest a second movie. He agrees. And he doesn't seem to mind when I move closer.

Even when I lean over toward him to get more comfortable.

He puts an arm around me, and it feels better than anything I can remember.

This man is nothing I believed him to be before. He's deep and kind and complex and generous and scarred and so warm at the core.

Warmer than anything and anyone I've ever known.

And I want it. I want that warmth. I want to bury myself in it. Never come out.

The second movie ends, but neither of us move. He's gently fiddling with a piece of my hair, his arm still wrapped around me. I shift my position slightly so I can rub his chest over his shirt.

He grows very still. "Scarlett."

"What?" I move again, pressing myself against him more fully and tilting my head up so I can see his face.

"You know what."

"What's wrong with this?"

His face twists dramatically, like it's taking great effort to hold himself back. His eyes are hot and fond and needy. Hungry. "I understand that you don't have anyone else right now, but I'm not the kind of man who plays around."

"I'm not playing around." I'm not a particularly forward woman romantically or sexually. I usually wait for the man to make the moves. I might not understand everything that's happening here, but I understand this much. Arthur is never going to make a move. He's afraid it might be wrong.

So I'm the one who has to.

"Scarlett."

"Why is it so hard for you believe that I might want this?"

He sucks in a ragged breath. He's so tense he's almost shaking with it. "Scarlett."

I reach up to cup one of his cheeks with my palm. "Arthur, I thought you didn't think of me that way, so I've been telling myself not to get ideas. But I can see now that you *do* think of me that way. And so I can admit it. I've never felt for anyone else the way I feel for you."

He makes another sound in his throat, but this one

sounds more like release than restraint. He takes my face in both his hands and leans down into a kiss.

A thrilling joy slams into me, filling my head and drowning my chest and pulsing eagerly between my legs. I wrap one arm around his neck and push into the kiss, opening my lips and trying to suck his tongue into my mouth.

He responds with equal enthusiasm, grabbing a fistful of my hair and thrusting his tongue in a deliciously primitive rhythm.

My cheeks burn. Arousal aches. His body is big and solid and strong and so warm. Everything I've ever wanted. I can't help but rub myself against any part of him I can reach.

"Baby," he mumbles, pulling his mouth away but only to scatter little kisses over my chin and cheeks and jaw and back to my lips.

"Yes!" The word comes out with a gasp as one of his hands finds my breast over my top and caresses me there.

I work my way down his chest and abdomen until I can feel the tight bulge of his erection in his pants.

He grunts and gives a little pump of his hips into my touch. But then something changes.

He groans again—with a different resonance this time—and uses both hands to move me away from him. Heaves himself to his feet and takes two long, fast steps away from me. Stands with his back to me, breathing heavily.

"Arthur," I whimper.

"I'm sorry, bab—" He gives himself a shake. "I'm sorry. I can't— I shouldn't do that."

"You definitely should do that." I feel like I might burst into tears, but reality hasn't hit me fully yet. "Why are you still holding back?"

"I'm sorry." He won't even look at me. "I really am. But it's wrong."

Before I can get another word out, he strides out of the room, closing the door behind him.

～

PRESENT

I wake up, still drowning in the kiss, still stinging from the rejection.

For a few moments, I have no idea where I am or when I am, but I'm conscious of a male body beneath mine. I'm lying against him, my head on his chest, my ear against his heartbeat. One of his arms is holding me and the other is slowly stroking my hair.

It feels so good. Better than anything. After a few seconds, I know for sure it's Arthur. No one smells as good as him, a mix of soap and laundry with an undernote of something faintly spicy. No one's touch is as gentle as his, like he's ensuring I don't break.

No one else would feel so much like mine.

That final realization is irrational, a product of a confused and too needy brain. On its heels I once again experience all the sensations from that kiss—already starting to fade into the dark fog of my mind—and then all the hurt at his pushing me away.

It was another dream that felt real.

The lingering sense of rejection upsets me so much I choke on a sudden sob. "No. Arthur, please. Don't leave." I clutch at his shirt almost desperately. For a few seconds, I have no idea whether I'm existing in the current moment or in that intense dream.

"I'm not leaving, baby. I'm right here. I'm still right here." He sounds soothing and slightly confused.

I lift my head and blink up at his face, trying to make myself think clearly. "Oh."

"What's the matter? Were you dreaming again?" He reaches out to palm my cheek.

I lean into his warm hand. "I... I don't know." My mind is getting away from me again, and I can't trust it. A dream is just a dream no matter how real it felt. "Were we... were we kissing?"

He's been half sitting, half lounging on the couch with me draped on top of him. But now he straightens up slightly. "No. Of course not. We were watching the movie and you fell asleep."

"Oh." The memory is clarifying now—tonight's

memory, the real one—but it's still too mingled with the dream to sort out completely.

"I'm sorry." He straightens up even more until he's in a sitting position. By necessity, I have to sit up too. "I shouldn't have been holding you like that without knowing whether it's what you want. I should have—"

"Stop, Arthur. You didn't do anything wrong. I leaned against you before I fell asleep. I... I liked it. It's not about that at all."

His expression relaxes visibly. "Okay. Good. Did you have a bad dream then? About... about me?"

"I don't know what it was." I collapse against him again, hating the complete mess of my brain at the moment, wishing it would behave the way it's supposed to. "I'm all confused."

Arthur wraps both arms around me and settles me more comfortably. I'm not on top of him as fully as I was before, but it still feels so nice. So needed. "It's okay. You were asleep. Do you think you were...?" He clears his throat with a weird sound. "Were you remembering something?"

"I don't think so. I think it was just a dream, and I can't even remember the details of it anymore. Everything is all jumbled in my head."

"Okay. Well, don't worry about it. Don't try to force it. Remember what the doctor said about letting your memories come back naturally."

"Yeah." I sigh and rub my face against his shirt. It's thick and soft, and it smells just like him. The chest beneath it is firm. Breathing a little faster than normal. His heart is racing.

He runs his hand down my loose hair and then settles it on the small of my back, rubbing in tight circles there.

It feels so good I release a soft moan. Flush at the embarrassing sound but then hear myself doing it again.

"Are you okay with this?" Arthur murmurs, his voice slightly thick.

"Yeah." I snuggle into him. "Feels good."

"Good. Just try to relax."

"Yeah." I close my eyes and enjoy the feel of his hand.

"You haven't been getting enough rest."

"Yes, I have."

"You've been through a lot. You need more rest than normal. Try to take it easy for the next couple of days."

"Mm-hmm." My body is heavy again. Pleasant darkness is rising behind my eyes. And nothing has ever felt as good as the firm caress of his hand on my back. "Feels so good."

"Yeah?"

"Yeah." I'm barely aware of what I'm saying now. "Love being touched like this. Been a long time since anyone touched me."

His hand moves higher, caressing my neck and head. "Has it?"

"Yeah. Long, long time."

"I know how that feels."

"Do you?" I'm fighting to stay awake, to make sense of this conversation. "So no one touches you either?"

"Not in a long time."

"What about your girlfriends?"

He exhales a short huff. "What girlfriends?"

"Don't you have girlfriends?" I'm sure I recall some talk about him dating, but maybe that was just in my dream.

"Not for a long time. I used to date. I wanted sex, and I wanted some sort of connection. But it was always empty until..."

"Until what?" I rub my cheek against his shirt again, too lethargic to make any other gestures of comfort.

"It felt empty. Even when I was trying to make it real, it felt empty. Eventually the emptiness was worse than being alone, so I stopped trying."

"You shouldn't be alone. You're too good to be alone."

"I'm not that good."

"Yes, you are." I squeeze him, wanting him to know I mean it. In the process, my forearm brushes up against something hard and intriguing and exciting in his lap. I move against it again, sleepily eager.

"Okay," he says, moving abruptly in a way that jars me out of my investigations. "That's enough of that."

"But I wanted to—"

"I know. But you're half-asleep, and even if you weren't,

you need to be mentally clear enough to make that decision. You're confused, so it's not going to happen. I might not be good, but I'm not *that* bad."

I keep trying to cling to him even as he stands up. "You are good."

"Thank you for believing that. Come on, baby. Let's get you to bed." He leans over, reaching for me, and before I know what's happening, he's lifted me up and settled me in his arms.

"You're carrying me?" I ask foolishly, wrapping an arm around him and lolling my head against his shoulder. I can't remember ever being carried like this. Not since I was a child.

"Yes, I'm carrying you. I'm not completely decrepit yet."

"You're not decrepit. You're nice and strong."

He chuckles at that as he starts to walk out of the room.

"What about Fred?" I ask, suddenly remembering the beloved dog who has been sound asleep on the couch all this time.

"He can come with you." He makes a short whistle between his teeth. "Come on, boy. You come to bed too."

I hear a scuffle that must be Fred jumping to the ground. I peer fuzzily around Arthur's shoulder and see the dog following at his heels. "Good boy."

Fred pants happily. I lean my head against Arthur again as he strides down the hall and then up the back stairway.

We've reached my bedroom when I ask groggily, "Did you call me baby?"

"Of course not." He lowers me onto the bed. Pulls off my slippers. Then adjusts the bedding so he can pull the sheet and duvet up over me.

"You didn't call me baby?" I'm sure I remember it. But all my memories now are fragmented and confusing.

He leans over and presses a kiss against my forehead. "Maybe you dreamed it."

"Maybe." I scoot over to make more room for Fred beside me. He turns three circles and then curls up in a ball on top of the covers near my right hip. "Thanks for carrying me."

He's rather breathless. I'm not tiny, and he carried me a long way. But he smiles down at me and murmurs, "Good night, Scarlett."

"Good night."

7

PAST

THE TWO WEEKS AFTER MY BROKEN KISS WITH ARTHUR ARE miserable.

Long and frustrating and tedious and *miserable*.

He barely talks to me at all.

It's obvious to me that it's about the kiss, about how he thinks it's wrong but wants to do it anyway. And that makes it even more upsetting—because he's pulled away for irrational reasons instead of letting us discover what this thing between us might be.

It might be nothing. It might be that our differences are impossible to overcome. Or it might be primarily physical attraction that goes nowhere. But I'm feeling more than that, and maybe he is too.

I'd like to try. See what could happen.

And he doesn't.

So I do my best to focus on work and try not to brood. As Dr. Walters keeps saying, I can't control other people. I can only control my own choices. Despite my hurt and utter exasperation with Arthur, I manage not to fall apart.

I keep hoping he'll come to his senses, but he doesn't.

It makes me want to shake him. Berate him for how stupid he's acting. Throw a temper tantrum and storm around.

I don't do any of that. It's not in my nature. I pull it all into a tight little ball inside as I calmly go through my daily routines.

I still see Arthur in passing, but he doesn't eat with me anymore. The first week and a half, he still takes me to my counseling appointments, but he only briefly replies when I try to initiate conversation, so the rides there and back are painfully awkward.

On the second Thursday after the kiss, he calls for a car service to take me.

It's the final blow. After ranting to Dr. Walters about the man's depravity for forty-five minutes, she quietly suggests I talk to him.

I've tried. More than once. He shuts down conversation.

She asks if I've directly brought up the kiss.

Of course I haven't. That would be making myself completely vulnerable. I never do that—just like I never make a fuss or cause a scene.

Dr. Walters says I can accept Arthur's decision without a fight, or I can take a difficult step. Do I really want to live the rest of my life not even trying to pursue my own happiness? Isn't that what I've spent twenty-seven years doing—letting other people maneuver me into what they thought was best instead of what was actually right for me? Has all the progress I've made in the months since my father died meant nothing?

The questions make me cry because I know the answers. I know what I have to do.

But I'm terrified.

On the ride home, I rehearse scenarios for what I could say and how I should say it. When I arrive, Arthur is in his home office with the door closed.

I stand in the hallway for several minutes, occasionally raising my hand to knock, but I never do. It's still work hours. Maybe he's legitimately busy. Interrupting him during an important call or project is hardly the way to make my point.

Knowing in the back of my mind these rationalizations are primarily an excuse for delay, I finally turn and walk away without knocking.

I work later than normal, telling myself I should make

up time but again finding a justification for not acting. Stella brings my dinner to the library. When she comes to pick up the tray and sees it's mostly uneaten, she asks me if I'm feeling all right and if there's anything she can do for me.

"I'm okay. I think."

She glances toward the hallway. Opens her mouth like she's going to say something. But doesn't.

I know the feeling. "Is he okay?" I ask, the unspokenness of the whole thing driving me crazy.

She shakes her head, her eyes still slanted in the direction of Arthur's office down the hall. "I don't know that he is."

I gulp. My annoyed frustration transforms into deep anxiety.

Arthur has as much baggage as I do. Maybe more since he's had a lot more years to collect it. I've managed to not fall apart, but maybe he hasn't.

And he's hiding in his office where no one can help him.

"Maybe you could check on him," Stella says softly. "I think he needs it."

I might never have summoned the necessary courage without the sudden wave of fear and concern for him. The urgency pushes me to my feet. I sway slightly and hold on to the edge of the desk.

"I know he's done it to himself," Stella adds, her blue

eyes very kind as they rest on my face. "But he needs you, dear."

And that's enough. Enough to compel me toward the door of the library and then down the hall to Arthur's office.

I tap on the door before I can talk myself out of it.

There's no answer from inside, so I knock again, louder this time.

"Go away, Stella." The voice is muffled, gruff.

I open the door and step inside.

One wall of his office is lined with bookcases, and there's a huge, antique desk in the middle of the floor. The only other furniture is a leather couch facing a fireplace.

It's a cool, damp night, but the temperature in the house is comfortable. There's certainly no reason for Arthur to have lit a fire. He's on the couch now, leaning forward toward the blaze in the fireplace, a whiskey glass in one hand.

He doesn't turn to see who entered. He mutters, "I don't need dinner or another lecture."

"Well, you clearly need something," I say tartly. "Because this is ridiculous."

His reaction to my voice is dramatic. He jerks so much he slops some of the whiskey in his glass. "What are you doing here?"

"I came to check on you." With a surge of confidence, I walk over and sit down beside him on the couch.

Recovered from his surprise, he leans forward again like he's not even allowing himself to get comfortable. His skin is damp with a sheen of perspiration and his hair is loose, wildly rumpled. His scar stands out starkly in the orange light of the fire. "I don't need checking on."

"Everyone who knows you would disagree with that assessment."

His mouth curls up in a faint snarl. "Can a man not be left alone for an evening?"

"You've been left alone for two weeks. In fact, you've been left alone for most of your life. Look what it's done for you. Absolutely nothing."

He exhales deeply, swirling the liquid in his glass. He hasn't looked at me directly since I entered. "Scarlett."

"Yes?"

"Please go away."

"No."

He blinks and slowly turns his head toward me. His brown eyes glint in the flickering light.

I arch my eyebrows. "I'm not going away. If you don't want to talk, we can just sit here all night and say nothing."

"There's nothing to say."

"I think there is."

"I thought you understood—"

"I understood what you were trying to tell me by pushing me away, but I don't accept it. You shouldn't either. It can't be the right decision if it makes you this miserable."

"I'm not—"

"You *are* miserable. Arthur, give me a little credit for having a brain. When I first moved here, you mostly kept to yourself, but you weren't all broody like this. You were kind of standoffish but also thoughtful and polite. You never rebuffed me or Stella or Billy. You weren't like *this*."

His jaw works tightly. His shoulders are visibly tense. He sucks in a breath, then glances at me and releases it again.

"Just say it, Arthur."

"It's easier..." He makes a huffing sound and clears his throat. "It was easier before I knew what I was missing."

It takes a few moments for his words to process in my mind. Then I make a guttural sound of surprise and sympathy.

He takes a swallow of whiskey, staring at the fire. "I've been alone almost all my life. But it's been ages since I've felt this lonely."

"Oh my God, Arthur, you're not alone now! You don't have to be lonely."

"Yes, I do."

"No, you don't. I'm sitting right here."

"I know that," he rasps. "But that makes it worse. Not better."

That would have hurt had I not known what he meant. "It's not wrong."

"Yes, it is. You don't need to be shackled to a damaged

old man who's never had a real relationship in his life. I'll never allow it. I'll live in misery for the rest of my life before I allow it."

"Oh my God, Arthur." I'm torn between indignation and a ridiculously swoony wave of excitement.

Because I had an idea of what was prompting Arthur's decline, but I hadn't realized his feelings for me were so serious.

It's clear he doesn't only want to kiss me. He wants a lot more.

"You've worked yourself up into a laughable melodrama here."

He shoots me a narrow-eyed glare.

"Don't give me that look. If you'd take even the slightest step back, you'd see how it's all gotten exaggerated in your mind. You're not an old man, and I'm just as damaged as you are."

"You are n—"

"Yes, I am. Everyone is damaged in their own way. It doesn't mean we don't deserve love. It doesn't mean we can never be happy."

He's staring down at the fire again. Says between his teeth, "I'm not going to do that to you, Scarlett."

With a stifled groan, I mentally sort through options, then say matter-of-factly, "Fine. You don't have to kiss me again. You can at least talk to me."

He blinks, clearly taken by surprise. He turns his head slowly.

"We don't have to do anything else. Why can't we at least be friendly like we were before?"

"Because every time you're close to me, I want to drag you to bed and bury myself inside you. I can't keep my hands off you. If we talk, I'm going to eventually turn it into something more."

My cheeks burn. My breath hitches. "Well... um... that's okay then. I won't mind if you feel the need to do that."

He frowns.

I reach over and gently pull the whiskey glass out of his hand. "You've probably had enough of this."

"It was just my first."

This time I'm the one surprised. "Really?"

"Yeah. I don't drink much. Not after my dad."

His dad would occasionally get drunk and hit him. That's what he told me. Of course he's not going to want to do anything that reminds him of that.

"Well, still. You don't need the drink. You need some fresh air." I stand up, reaching down to give one of his arms a little tug.

He doesn't move. "I don't need fresh air. I need to be left alone."

"You're acting like a child in a pout, and it's not like you at all. Let's take a walk."

He growls low in his throat. "Scarlett, go the fuck away."

I stare down at him, suddenly hit with a blinding realization.

I've been waiting for him to explode. Lose control of his temper. Let loose in anger and frustration. My father never hit me, but he was fiery, and when he was angry, he got very loud. He would snap and yell at me, and I'd be totally cowed, crying in my room until the following day when we would both pretend it never happened.

A little part of me has been waiting for Arthur to snap in the same way, but it's not going to happen. Even in anger, he's under control.

He's never going to yell at me. He's never going to cow me. He's never going to make me feel as helpless as my father did.

Even right now, at his worst, he makes me strong.

His eyebrows lower. "What's the matter, baby?" he asks hoarsely, immediately dropping his own brooding out of concern for me.

I make a silly sobbing sound at the naked worry on his face and at the endearment. "Nothing. Everything is good. I'm good." I'm more than good. I'm washed with a thrilling kind of power I've never experienced before. "Come on and take a walk with me."

"We can't do anything else."

"Fine. Nothing else. Just a walk."

That placates him enough. When I tug at his arm again, this time he heaves himself to his feet. But he jerks and grunts as he straightens up, his face twisting in pain.

"What's the matter?" I ask, reaching for him like he needs support.

He gives his head a quick shake. "Nothing. Just a catch in my back." Despite his downplaying of it, he has visible difficulty standing up straight, and his breathing is slightly ragged.

"Well, no wonder if you've been sitting like this for a long time. Leaning over like that is terrible on your back. You need to stretch it out. Walking might help."

He gives a low grumble in his throat, but this time it sounds like his put-on grumpiness rather than a genuine bad mood. He manages to stand straight, and we walk slowly out of the office, down the hall, and then outside.

After a while, I slide an arm around his waist. His back is hurting, and he needs support.

He doesn't exactly lean on me, but he also doesn't pull away.

I'll take it.

The next day I wake up excited. Hopeful. Looking forward to seeing Arthur again today.

It feels like something has changed, and this is

confirmed when he wanders into the breakfast room while I'm eating my bagel and scanning my phone. He gets a cup of coffee and sits down across from me at the table, murmuring good morning before he opens one of the three newspapers that are always stacked neatly on a side table.

He used to do this all the time, but lately he's been drinking his coffee and reading the newspaper in his office. No doubt to avoid me.

"How's your back?" I ask when I see him shifting uncomfortably in his seat.

"Fine." He gives me a little smile. "Thanks."

I smile back, trying not to melt away at the barely restrained warmth of his expression. "It looks like it's still bothering you."

"It'll be fine. I just need to stretch it out."

I have no reason to doubt that is true, but I wish I could do something to fix it for him.

He needs someone to take care of him, and he's never really had anyone.

He needs someone.

He needs *me*.

I should be shocked by my confidence, my absolute surety in this, but there's no doubting the clear entitlement that's settled in my heart sometime between last night and right now.

Arthur is mine to take care of. Somehow I've got to break through the last of his walls so he'll let me.

I think about it during the day as I work, mentally playing out various ideas and discarding most of them as ineffective or too far out of character for me to manage.

When I wrap up my work at a little after five in the afternoon, I wander down the hall to his office. The door is open, which is a relief, but he's not in the room when I peek inside.

Frowning, I keep walking, checking the dining room and the sitting room and the media room and coming up empty.

I end up in the kitchen, peering around and only seeing Stella, who is standing over a big pot on the stove. "Beef stew," she says when she notices me. "It still needs at least another hour and a half."

"Smells delicious."

She must see something on my face because her expression changes slightly. "He's up in his bedroom."

"What is he doing up there at five thirty?" I mutter, mostly to myself. I turn to leave, waving my thanks to Stella, who is now chuckling to herself.

I head upstairs and tap on his bedroom door.

There's no response.

Frowning, I knock again, and again there's no response.

This is ridiculous. He was better this morning. He wasn't closing me out. I'm not going to let him slam another door in my face just when I was making a little progress.

So I take a deep breath and open the door.

The room appears empty. Nothing but his big bed with its walnut four-poster frame, a long dresser, and the small sitting area over by the bay window. But the door to the attached bathroom is half-open, and from it I hear the unmistakable sound of music—some sort of dramatic classical stuff I don't recognize—and spraying water.

Oh. He's taking a shower.

It's definitely not his normal routine, but it's a completely harmless thing for him to be doing right now. I'll give him some time and then come to find him. Maybe we can have dinner together and hang out this evening.

I've turned to leave when I hear something else. It's almost drowned by the music and the shower sprays, but I recognize it. A long, soft, hoarse, sustained groan.

Arthur.

My mind immediately jumps into crisis mode. Maybe his back gave out. Or he slipped in the shower. He might be hurt. I absolutely have to check. The man is so proud and stubborn that he might not even ask for help when injured.

I hurry to the doorway and look inside. His bathroom is even bigger than the one in my suite, with two marble-topped vanities in dark wood, large silver-framed mirrors, a separate room for the toilet, and a huge glass-enclosed shower with walls tiled beautifully in various shades of gray.

Arthur is indeed in the shower, facing away from me, toward the wall. The music and the sound of water are both significantly louder from in here, and he clearly has no idea of my presence. The glass walls of the enclosure are starting to get foggy but not enough to disguise his naked body.

His long hair is plastered wetly around his neck and shoulders. His strong back tapers down to lean hips and a deliciously tight butt. His legs are long, but soon my attention moves elsewhere.

He's leaning over slightly, bracing against the tile wall with one hand. The other hand is moving in a fast, choppy motion, just lower than his middle.

I can't actually see that hand or his groin, but there's no question what he's doing.

As I stare, he releases another one of those groans.

If sex had a voice, it would be that long, thick moan.

My whole body goes hot. Arousal pulses achingly between my thighs. I'm turned on so intensely and so quickly I can barely take a full breath.

His hand is speeding up. His body tightening. His ass cheeks make small rhythmic clenches.

He jerks his head up and pushes hard against the tile with his bracing hand. Bites out "Scarlett" just before his body shudders with release.

He's making pleased, gaspy sounds when I finally come back to my senses.

What the hell am I doing? This is an intensely private act, and he has no idea that I'm here. I'm spying on him like a gangly adolescent, too immature to recognize boundaries.

I turn on my heel and hurry out of the bathroom and then out of his bedroom. Guilty and flustered and in a panic, I run all the way down the hall to my suite, throwing myself into my room and closing the door behind me.

Oh my God.

That was probably the hottest, most erotic moment of my life. I've had sex before, and it was good, but it never made me feel like *this*.

But it was wrong. I never should have witnessed what I saw. And I absolutely have to stop visualizing it now.

He said my name right before he came. I know I didn't imagine that.

He was thinking about me when he was doing all that.

Despite my good intentions, my brain fixates on the scene, reviewing every detail of what I saw and reliving it again and again. The repeated fantasy does nothing to clear my mind. It only turns me on even more. After a few minutes, I'm so aroused that I can't lie still.

My body is pulsing. My skin is flushed all the way down to my stomach. I know what I need. It's been a long time since I've had sex. I haven't even masturbated since all the shit blew up with my dad, and I'm aching for a release.

I get up to lock my bedroom door before I climb back on the bed and stare up at the ceiling, panting.

I imagine Arthur in the shower again, his hand pumping, his ass clenching. I hear him moaning out my name.

I make a little whimpering sound and rub my breasts over my top. Imagine he's the one touching me.

My nipples peak under my bra. The garment feels too binding, so I reach under my shirt to unhook it and then pull it off. I don't get naked when I do this. It makes me too self-conscious. But the bra has to come off.

I touch myself more, lingering on my breasts before sliding a hand down to tuck under the waist of my pants so I can rub my clit over my underwear.

I hear myself making a sensual groan as the pleasure coils tightly. My hand speeds up, rubbing hard circles at my clit as my other hand tweaks one of my nipples.

It feels so good I arch my spine and squirm my hips. I lick my lips and toss my head. The pleasure is intense and visceral, but it tightens endlessly without releasing. I give a ragged sob as I start to pump my hips, but it's still not enough.

When the erotic pressure becomes torturous, I turn over onto my stomach. Adjust my knees to lift my butt higher than the rest of me.

For some reason I've never understood, I can't seem to bring myself to orgasm unless my ass is in the air.

I used to be ashamed—turning out all the lights, locking the door, panting silently against the pillow as I'd bring myself to a hot, fast climax. But I don't feel ashamed anymore. I'm not sure I've ever been so turned on.

I don't touch myself immediately, just stay poised like that, my butt raised up, my cheek against the duvet, and visualize Arthur saying my name as he comes.

With a stifled whimper, I finally can't resist any longer. I slide my hand up between my legs and under my pants and panties until I can feel how wet I am. I'm so into it that I push my clothes halfway down my legs so my butt is bare, hit deliciously by the cool air of the room. I thrust with my middle finger until it feels so good I can't hold back the little grunts forcing their way out of my throat.

Then I give my clit a series of little slaps with my other hand, rocking my body with each impact, until I'm sobbing into the bedding with the intensity of my orgasm.

I shift my slaps to rubbing until I come again, not quite as hard as before but just as satisfying.

I stay in position until the spasms completely fade. Then I flop over onto my side, gasping and shuddering as my body relaxes completely.

When I've recovered, I giggle a little as I pull up my pants and panties. I really can't believe I just did that. It's not like me at all.

But it felt so good, and I'm so relaxed now I'm tempted to pull the covers up and go to sleep.

I'm on the verge of drifting off when there's a knock on my bedroom door. I sit up abruptly in a sudden panic even though I rationally know no one could possibly know what I just did.

"Scarlett?" It's Arthur. "Are you in there?"

"Yes, I'm here." My voice cracks. It still sounds like I'm breathless.

"Are you okay?" He's genuinely concerned now.

"I'm fine!"

"You don't sound fine. What's going on? Can I come in?"

"Yes. Of course." I reply that because it's the only way for me to sound normal.

The doorknob turns a few times.

Then I remember I locked it.

"Oh, hold on," I say, jumping up and hurrying to the door. I unlock it and swing it open. "Sorry."

He's not long out of his shower. His hair is wet and pulled back. He's got on a T-shirt and old gray sweats. "What's the matter?" He scans my face urgently. "You look flushed. Are you sick?"

Before I can stop him, he reaches out and feels my forehead, then slides his palm down to cup one of my cheeks. "You feel warm. Do you have a fever?"

"No, I don't have a fever!" I can't believe this is happening. How did I get myself into this ridiculous situation? "I'm fine. Just a little warm, I guess. I was..." I fumble mentally for an excuse to have the door locked. "I was on the phone."

He's still frowning. If I didn't know better, I'd have no idea what he was doing in the shower not very long ago. "Who were you talking to on the phone?"

"What does it matter?" I sound grumpy because I'm running out of excuses, and I really want him to let it go.

His forehead lowers. His eyes darken. "Why won't you tell me? And why are you so flushed? Were you talking to a boyfriend?"

He's now offered me a perfect excuse for what I was doing just now, but there's no way I can take it. "Of course I don't have a boyfriend! What the hell, Arthur? Do you think if I had a boyfriend I'd be... I'd be this way with you?"

His shoulders and his jaw relax. His eyes deepen. "What way is that?"

"You know what way," I grumble. "You know exactly what I'm talking about. Of course I don't have a boyfriend."

"Okay." He shifts his weight from foot to foot almost imperceptibly. "Good."

"Yes."

His mouth twitches faintly. "I'm glad. I wouldn't like that at all."

"Wouldn't you?" I've completely forgotten my embarrassment. Nothing matters but that fond look in his eyes. "Why wouldn't you like it?"

"You know why."

"I thought you said it was wrong and you wouldn't do it."

"That doesn't mean I want some other asshole to get his hands on you."

I can't help giggling at that. "If I had a boyfriend, he wouldn't be an asshole."

"I beg to differ." He sounds cool. Lofty. Teasing. "So if it wasn't an asshole boyfriend, who were you on the phone with? Are you sure you're not getting sick?" He reaches over to feel my forehead again.

Despite the brief boyfriend diversion, he's completely in control now. I honestly can't believe he was jerking off in the shower not very long ago. Something needs to shake this man out of his endless composure.

Maybe I'm the one who has to do it.

Once the temptation arises, it won't be denied.

"If you must know, I was getting myself off." The words come out blandly. I hear them. I actually say them.

Arthur freezes with his lips parted slightly. Only his eyes move, searching my face.

"So no, I'm not getting sick."

He starts to say something, but no sound comes out.

I stifle a giggle. "Are you finally at a loss for words? I never thought I'd see the day."

He opens his mouth again. Makes a weird guttural sound.

"All right then." I'm not sure how to bring this topic to a close, so hopefully he'll remember how to speak again soon.

"Scarlett," he finally rasps.

"What?" I blink at him in exaggerated innocence.

"Don't tell me that!"

"Why not?"

"I'm having a hard enough time controlling myself around you as it is." There's a fire in his eyes now that he's always trying to hide. It's blazing hotly. "I don't need that visual to compound it."

"Oh." I blush again, pleased and just a little self-conscious. "Sorry about that."

Both of us know I'm not sorry at all.

8

PAST

FOR THE ENTIRE WEEK AFTER I SAW HIM IN THE SHOWER, WE go through our daily routines, alternating between playful teasing and warm bonding.

I never push him to kiss me again, although I occasionally remind him it's what I want. It's a boundary he's set for himself. Even though it's irrational, he takes it seriously, and I'm not going to plow over his choices or try to seduce him into forgetting them.

I want to be with him, but he needs to want it too— freely and unreservedly. Until he does, there's nothing I can do but enjoy him in any way I'm allowed.

Inexplicably, I'm happier this week than I can ever

remember being before. I might not have everything I want, but I have real companionship, fellowship, emotional intimacy.

I'm safe with him to be myself. I don't have to always be nice and agreeable and perfectly pleasant.

I can simply be me and trust that he's not going to blow up on me, reject me, or use me for his own purposes.

It's freeing. Thrilling.

I might be wrong, but I think Arthur has never been happier either.

On Saturday evening a week later, Stella prepares us a dinner out on the back patio because the weather has turned warm and pleasant. She sets the table beautifully with silver, crystal, and flowers, and she lights candles in big glass globes all around the table.

It's the most romantic setting I've ever experienced. I'm speechless as I gaze around and then join Arthur at the table.

He's standing beside his chair, half smiling in that wry way he has. "I think Stella got carried away."

"It's beautiful. I love it."

He can't seem to look away from my face. "All right," he murmurs. "Then I won't complain."

He helps me into my seat and then pours the wine. Stella brings out salmon and salad and risotto and fresh-baked bread. She's hiding a smile as she serves our meals with extra decorum. I'd swear she's almost as giddy as me.

Arthur and I chat about the books I'm currently working on, and he tells me about his time in college and how he always wanted to go to graduate school and study history or philosophy but his father made it clear he had no choice but to manage the family's assets—so vast and complex it's always been a full-time job for the Worthing heir.

"Can't you reorganize things?" I ask at last.

"What do you mean?"

"I mean can't you reorganize things so you don't have to be so hands-on? I know all that stuff needs active management, but do you really have to do all of it yourself? I guess I don't really know what all that work consists of. I assume you're not just moving money around. Are you running companies your family owns? Can't you put other people in leadership roles in those companies?"

"They already have leadership in place. But everything has been structured so that the Worthing in charge is the final decision-maker on everything."

I make a face. "That seems like nonsense."

His eyes narrow.

"I'm not trying to be mean, but isn't that just a remnant of the past rather than an inevitable fact of existence? Can't you change it?"

He's looking at me strangely. Almost like he's never even considered the possibility before. "Why would I?"

"So you could do something else. Something that would make you happy."

"I'm forty-six, baby. It's a little late for a new career."

"Why would it be? You might be only halfway through your life. Why spend the rest of it doing work you don't even like?"

"It's not that bad. I've done a decent job."

"I'm sure you have. You're so smart you could do anything you set your mind to, but that doesn't mean you have to do it. Give the folks in leadership more authority. You could even sell some stuff off to make it more manageable."

He looked as pleased as a boy at the compliment, but his expression shifts as he considers my suggestions. "Generations of Worthings would turn over in their graves."

"So let them. They can't do anything about it now." I hesitate before I summon the courage to add, "Your dad can't control you anymore."

He winces and jerks his head to the side. Then his shoulders rise and fall in an extended breath. "Yeah."

"You could go back to school."

His eyebrows shoot up. "What?"

"Graduate school. Like you always wanted. Or you could do something else if you'd rather. Write a book. Start your own business. If you weren't tied down by all these chains of the Worthing past, you'd be free to do anything. Anything."

His face works strangely. "It sounds too good to be true."

"It's not. It would take an adjustment, I'm sure, and some planning, but it's got to be doable. What about your cousins?"

"What about them?"

"You have a bunch, don't you? Maybe they'd want to be involved and take leadership."

"A couple already are."

"Well, there you go. Work with them to figure something out. You've spent all this time hiding from life, but you don't have to do it forever." I reach over and cover his hand, which is fiddling with his dessert spoon. "Do you?"

It takes him a long time to respond. I wait as his internal debate processes in his expression. Finally he says in a rasp, "I guess maybe I don't."

We smile at each for so long I'm afraid I might drown in it. Stella saves us by coming out with my favorite chocolate mousse for dessert.

After we finish, I'm not ready for the evening to end, so I suggest a walk. Arthur readily agrees. We wander the gardens and grounds, talking about possibilities for Arthur's future career. At one point, he reaches over to take my hand and doesn't relinquish it.

So we hold hands for the rest of the walk.

It's dark by the time we finally return to the house. We

stand on the patio next to the table Stella has already cleared and just look at each other.

"Arthur?" I ask at last.

He swallows visibly. Inclines his head in his brief nod.

I suck in a breath. "Does that mean…?"

"I'm tired of hiding from life. I'm tired of not allowing myself anything I want for fear it will end up hurting me. I'm tired of always being haunted by the ghost of my father. I don't want to do it anymore."

"Then don't." I step closer. Reach up to grab a handful of his shirt. "Don't do it anymore."

"I want to…" He exhales a shaky breath, almost a dry laugh. "I want to live."

"Then do it." I lean closer, tilting my face up toward his. "Do it, Arthur. *Live.*"

He groans. His expression cracks. He takes my face in both his hands and leans down into a kiss.

I respond immediately, still clutching at his shirt with one hand and reaching up to grip his ponytail with the other. I'm bombarded with wave after wave of pleasure and excitement—but also that deeper sense of ownership.

It's been growing day by day, and I've never been able to shake it.

I doubt I ever will.

We kiss until it's entirely inappropriate behavior for a patio where Stella or Billy might wander by. Arthur's got me pushed up against the half-wall surround, and one of his hands is between my legs.

He's always been so completely controlled I wouldn't have expected him to lose it quite so quickly, but he seems to have forgotten where we are.

"Maybe we should take this upstairs," I manage to gasp when he breaks the kiss to mouth his way down my throat.

He jerks and grows still like he's trying to make his mind work. Then he huffs as he pulls his hand out from between my thighs. "Good thinking." His cheeks have darkened. His hair was pulled back at the nape of his neck, but half of it has escaped messily out of the ponytail. His eyes look even darker than normal. He gives me a wry, clever smile.

He's the sexiest thing I've ever seen.

"Let's definitely go upstairs. Fast."

He chuckles at that and takes my hand as we walk inside and then down the hall and up the stairs. We reach his room first, so that's where we go. By mutual agreement, we start working on our clothes, pulling off our shoes and socks. I take off the light cardigan I'm wearing while he pulls off his watch and then takes off his shirt, dragging his white undershirt off over his head afterward.

I stare at his bare chest, distracted from disrobing by

the sight. His arms and shoulders are nicely developed, but his abdomen is slightly soft. Irresistibly touchable.

He sees me staring and glances down at himself. "Disappointed?"

"Not even close." I move toward him, reaching out so I can squeeze the extra flesh on his sides.

That makes him laugh again as he unhooks his belt. I'm watching as he unfastens his pants and pushes them down his legs, pulling them off so he's left wearing nothing but a pair of black boxer briefs. He's already hard. I can see the shape of his erection beneath the snug fabric.

My heart is racing with excitement now, and my breathing is uneven. I love the sight of him. I want to touch him all over and have him touch me. But I'm also a little nervous. It's been a while since I've had sex, and I've never been particularly skilled or adventurous.

What if I can't give him what he wants? What if I'm not what he wants me to be?

"Scarlett, what's wrong?" His tone is different than it was. Soft and serious.

I shake my head, my throat tightening over any answer I might give him.

"Are we moving too fast?" He's tilting his head slightly, searching my face. "Do you want to slow down?"

Again I shake my head and this time manage to say, "No. I definitely want this."

A tension I hadn't been aware of relaxes in his shoulders and in his expression. "Okay. That's good then. So what—?"

"I'm just nervous," I blurt out. "I'm sorry. I know it's very unsexy, but I suddenly got nervous."

His eyes soften. "You think I'm not?"

"No. Why would you be? You're smart and suave and sexy and—"

"And laughably out of practice at this."

"It's been a while since I've had sex too."

"However long it's been for you, I can guarantee it's been longer for me. I'll do everything I can to please you, but I hope you're not expecting the most impressive performance."

A snicker surprises me. I raise a hand to cover my mouth.

He smiles and steps over so he can cup my face in both his hands. "Baby, you don't have anything to worry about. Just being with you is more than I ever imagined. If we don't get things quite right the first time, we'll try again. We'll talk it through and figure it out. Just be honest with me."

"I have been."

He inclines his head in that little nod. "So you have absolutely no doubts about being with me like this?"

His openness is calming my flutters of fear. It's impossible not to believe he wants this. He wants me. His main concern is that I'll be the one who's disappointed. "I want this, Arthur. I've never wanted anything more."

With a guttural sound, he leans into another kiss. This one is just as urgent and deep as our kiss on the patio, but nothing interrupts us this time. He walks us toward the bed until the back of my legs hit the frame. Then he leans down to fold over the duvet and hefts me up and lays me down so I'm on my back on the bed.

I reach out to pull him on top of me, and he claims my mouth again, thrusting his tongue deep and rocking his hips in the same sensual rhythm.

The bulge of his erection is pressing into my middle, and the feel of it makes me clench. I desperately need to pull him inside me. The ache of it makes me whimper.

After a few minutes, he straightens one arm and lifts his upper body to look down at me. "Can I take off your clothes?"

I'd actually forgotten I was still dressed. I never got any further than my shoes and sweater. "Yes! Sorry. I'm way behind you." I grab the bottom of my top and pull it up.

Arthur helps me get it over my head and then stares fixedly down at my white bra, which runs the midline between prettiness and practicality. He breathes something that sounds like "Scarlett."

I smile as I reach behind me to unhook the bra, pulling it away from my skin.

He makes a throaty sound at the sight of my bare

breasts, then uses one hand to caress them very gently. "Fuck."

I hear myself giggling. He appears to appreciate the sound. He smiles and leans to kiss me softly, eventually kissing his way down to my chest.

He spends a long time giving my breasts attention, so long that I can't hold back a lot of gasps and squirms as arousal rises quickly.

Eventually I get impatient and tug off my pants. It's a little awkward because of my prone position, but eventually we peel them off so I'm left wearing nothing but a little pair of white panties.

If I'd known I was going to end up in bed with Arthur today, I would have put on something sexier.

He clearly has no complaints. He moves lower down my body until he's nuzzling between my legs. I clutch at his hair as he tongues me through the damp cotton and make the most ridiculous whining sound when the sensations become too intense. "Arthur, please. I'm ready."

He straightens up onto his knees. "I've got condoms."

I lick my lips. "Yeah. That's smart. I'm not on birth control."

He reaches into the drawer of his nightstand and pulls out a packet. Then he stands up to shuck his underwear.

I leer shamelessly at the sight of him, his erection thick and hard as he rolls on the condom.

I slide out of my panties and gaze up at him as he climbs back onto the bed.

He reaches out and thumbs my bottom lip, rubbing it in a way that stimulates hundreds of nerve endings. Then he slides his hand down to trace the curve of my breasts before he moves it lower to caress my belly.

Then he finally reaches my groin. He strokes me open and slides one finger inside me. I'm wet. More than aroused. He makes a satisfied sound as he joins the first finger with another and pumps them a few times.

It feels good. I suck in a sharp breath as my spine arches up.

"You're so beautiful," he murmurs, his eyes running up and down my body. "I've never seen anyone I want more."

The words make me feel almost as good as his touch. My legs part automatically. I clutch the duvet folded on one side of me. "Me too, Arthur. Please. Don't make me wait anymore."

He climbs over my body, parting my legs to make room for him. Then he adjusts his position, staring hotly down at my body for a few seconds before he asks, "Is there anything in particular you like?"

I have a brief, breathless vision of him turning me over on my hands and knees, but it's not in me to actually ask for that at the moment. I believe he genuinely wants me. I believe he's all the way into this. But despite his lifetime-nurtured cynicism, he's a romantic at heart. He's going to expect me to want this sweet and safe.

"Is there something?" he prompts when I hesitate just a bit too long.

"This is perfect." I'm not lying. I like being able to see his face. I like how my arms can wrap around him in this position. I like how he's the one making things happen.

It's our first time. Surely this is more appropriate.

He bends his arms to lower his body enough to kiss me slow and soft. His movements are leisurely, delicate in a way that seems intentional. He explores my mouth with his tongue until I'm so turned on I have to wrap one leg around his thighs, trying to shift our positions enough to give me some friction on my clit.

He's smiling when he finally lifts his head. He presses little kisses around my mouth, on my cheekbones, down my neck.

It's soft and delicious and so incredibly gentle.

But does nothing to ease the overwhelming ache at my center.

"Arthur."

"You ready?"

"Yes. You don't have to be so careful. I'm dying here."

There's a flicker in the tight control on his face, but it passes too quickly for me to identify it. He repositions my legs, bending my knees more and pulling my thighs farther apart. Then he adjusts my bottom enough to line himself up at my entrance.

He's looking me in the eye when he guides himself inside me, penetrating an inch before pulling back out and sinking in farther at a slightly different angle.

It's been well over a year since I've had sex. I feel tighter than I'm used to, and while he's not unusually large, he's also not small and he fills me snugly.

I inhale sharply and lift my hips, trying to relax around the deepening pressure.

About halfway in, he jerks his head to the side, closing his eyes and breathing unevenly. He's already sweating despite his deliberateness. Muscles are tensing in his jaw and his neck.

"Are you okay?" I ask, distracted from the slight discomfort. I cup the side of his jaw with one hand.

He huffs a few times. It takes a moment for me to recognize it as dry laughter. "Yes. Trying not to embarrass myself."

I choke on a laugh too. "If I shouldn't be nervous, you shouldn't be embarrassed."

He's gotten ahold of himself now. He turns his head back to meet my eyes. "Good to know. I'd still like this to last longer than two seconds."

"Ah. Got it." I rub my palm against the rough stubble on his jaw. It's irresistibly scratchy. "Well, I don't mind going a second time. You should take your own advice. If we don't get things quite right, we'll try again."

"Honestly, I wasn't expecting to be this close to losing it so soon. But I think I've managed to get it together now. Crisis averted."

I shift my hips around the feel of his erection inside me. Big and tight and full and needed. I want to giggle at his tone, but a shiver of pleasure surprises me, so it comes out as a weird little whimper.

His eyes go hot.

"That was a good sound," I say rather foolishly.

"I know that."

He shifts his weight onto one of his arms, freeing the other to slide down my body so he's cupping my butt. He holds me there as he starts to thrust.

His initial rhythm is as careful as his earlier moves—steady and controlled and stimulating. I respond eagerly, bending my legs up around his hips and pumping my hips to match his motion.

It feels good. Incredibly good. The arousal pulsing inside me since the garden heightens and deepens and drives me crazy. Soon I'm making loud, hoarse pants as I work my body against his, chasing a release that's promised but not within reach.

I know he's watching me even in the midst of his own physical enjoyment. He shifts his angle a few times as he thrusts. He moves my legs so they're higher. His hand tightens on my ass, lifting me slightly. Sweat is dripping down the sides of his face now, dampening his hairline. His breathing has accelerated. His jaw and neck start to look tense again.

He's holding back. Waiting for me. He wants me to come. And I want that too. I make a frustrated sound as I drag my fingernails across the skin of his back, trying to ride him from below in an attempt to get there.

"Baby, what do you need?" He stops pumping his hips, growing still while inside me.

"I—" My face is blazing hot. It feels like my hair is a mess, sticking to my skin. "I'm good."

"Tell me what you need. Right now." This time he sounds almost stern.

Ridiculously, my body clenches in excitement at the tone. "We could try— I mean maybe... from behind."

Because I'm watching closely, I see a flash of heat on his face. But then his eyebrows draw together in a frown. "Why didn't you tell me what you like?"

"I didn't... I thought..." I have absolutely no excuse.

"Next time you tell me the truth." His voice has that firm, authoritative edge to it again. My channel clenches hard around his erection.

He slides out and straightens up so he's on his knees. "Now turn over."

I stare up at him, momentarily incapacitated by the wave of hot pleasure that's slammed into me.

"Scarlett. Turn over on your hands and knees. Do it now." He must have figured out a thing or two about what I like because he's never spoken to me that way before.

I do what he says, trembling and breathless.

My position is exposed, vulnerable. And more so when I bend my arms, resting on my forearms so my butt is higher than the rest of me.

I'm so excited now I can't hold back a little whimper.

He puts a hand between my shoulder blades, easing my upper body down even farther. Then he slides his palm to the small of my back. Over one of my butt cheeks and then the other. Along the crease until he's caressing my thighs.

"Is this what you like?" he asks thickly.

"Yes. Yes please. I need..."

"I'm going to give you what you need." He widens my knees and slides a finger inside me. I'm so wet it makes a suction sound.

He pumps one finger, then two, then three inside me, his speed accelerating gradually until he's fucking me hard with his hand. I whimper and gasp as all the arousal from the past hour gathers and tightens into a delicious coil.

He grips one side of my bottom with his free hand. "That's right. You're so hot and wet. You're getting tighter. Just let it come. You're taking it so well. Be good for me and come. You can do it, baby."

His voice is just as erotic as his touch. I climax before I

expect it, sobbing out the sudden surge of pleasure as my whole body shakes and my channel spasms hard around his fingers.

"That's right. That's so good. You're coming so beautifully. Keep going. Take everything you need."

His words and the way he keeps pushing against the contractions sustain the orgasm longer than it should reasonably last. When I've finally stop clenching, I'm gasping wetly against the mattress, my butt still high in the air and moisture dripping down my inner thigh.

He pulls his fingers out and strokes my thighs and ass with both hands. "Are you ready for more?"

"Yes. Please."

I hear him moving behind me, so I glance behind. He's checking the condom. Then he lifts himself higher on his knees and moves directly behind me. He pulls apart my butt cheeks and aligns his erection at my entrance, pushing in slowly, making me moan.

He presses my upper body down farther and then gathers my hair into one fist, holding it as he starts to thrust.

He's not as controlled as before. Maybe he's losing his restraint at last, or maybe he's figured out that's not what I want from him. He starts with a couple of long thrusts, but soon he's fucking me hard and fast, his groin slapping against my ass with every instroke.

He's shaking my body. Shaking the bed. I push back

against him, making helpless sounds that are stretched and almost childish as another climax builds.

He's talking me through it like before, murmuring out rough encouragement. "That's so good. You're taking it so well. You're gonna come again. Don't fight it. You're so beautiful. So hot. You're feeling so good. You can trust me. You can let go."

I'm sobbing again as another orgasm finally breaks. I'm too loud. Way too loud. But I can't seem to hold it back or even hide it in the bedding.

"That's right. So good. You're coming so good. This is what you've needed all this time."

He keeps talking until my spasms have faded and I'm making only little whimpers of satisfaction. The sheet beneath my face is damp from saliva and tears, and my entire groin is still pulsing with the aftermath. "You come too," I manage to gasp. "Arthur, you let go too." I twist my neck to see his face.

He's gazing down at me with a hot hunger that's almost primitive. He's holding himself very still.

"Please, Arthur. Let go."

He makes a guttural sound and starts to thrust again. Fast and tight and gripping my ass with both his hands. He starts to grunt like an animal, his expression twisting as he works toward release.

I keep looking back so I can see him. I see his face as he finally comes.

I've never seen anything like it.

He keeps bumping against my bottom as he rides out his climax, ending with a stretched exclamation that might have been "Baby."

We hold the position for a minute after he finally stops moving. Then he slides out and I collapse on my side.

He quickly takes care of the condom and then falls over beside me on the bed, pulling me to his side.

We lay together like that for a long time before we're capable of conversation.

"That was so good," I say at last, kissing his chest.

"Yeah. Yeah."

I peek up at his face. He's relaxed. Smiling slightly. Warm and fond and groggy. "Thank you."

He brushes a kiss into my hair. "You don't have to thank me. That was the hottest thing I've ever experienced."

"Me too."

"Good."

We're silent for a few more minutes until I need a little more reassurance. "So... so we can do it again?"

He huffs in tired amusement. "Definitely." He pulls me up so he can meet my eyes. "There's no pressure, Scarlett. We're just starting out. So we can take this as it comes and see what happens. But I definitely want to do that again."

I smile. I'd rather him blurt out his undying love for me, but I'm not a teenager or a fool. This is good. This is everything I should expect. "Good. Me too."

9

PRESENT

I WAKE UP IN A DARK ROOM ABSOLUTELY CONVINCED I JUST made love to Arthur.

I can still feel his hands on my body, his thrusting inside me, his low, thick voice vibrating through my blood.

I'm hot and panting and damp with perspiration, my covers tangled up around my limbs so much I'm momentarily trapped when I try to sit up.

My first instinct is to look at the other side of my bed, expecting to see Arthur's naked form. Maybe sleeping. Maybe awake and thoughtful and relaxed, watching me quietly.

He's not there. My chest tightens with an instinctive ache over the idea of his leaving without a word after we had sex, but finally my mind is starting to clear.

We didn't have sex. The last thing I distinctly remember is having dinner with Arthur on the couch as we watched movies. I dozed off. He carried me up. I was groggy and fell asleep immediately after, but I'm sure that much really occurred. Now I can recognize Fred at the bottom of the bed, stretched out and snoring softly.

Arthur was so kind and strong and gentle and reassuring this evening. I've never had a man treat me like that, make me feel so safe.

The sex that's filling my mind didn't happen. Not tonight. Not ever. It's some kind of wish fulfillment dream. The closer I get to Arthur, the more I want him physically. And now it's taken the form of intense, erotic dreams.

Even the vague remnants of the dream are enough to turn me on. I keep focusing on them, trying to hold on to them even as they fade, turn them into a complete story.

It's hopeless and only serves to arouse me to the point of desperation. I roll over, lift my bottom, and rub myself hard and fast over my panties until I come in quiet gasps against my pillow.

My body is more satisfied afterward, but not my mind.

There's something there, lurking on the edges of my consciousness, hidden by the dark, swirling fog of my brain.

It's terrible—this taunting blackness. It's torture.

I lie awake for a long time but come up with no answers.

Despite my late-night confusion, the week that follows is a good one.

A really good week.

It's one of the best I can remember.

Arthur is more present than he was before. Not so much the amount of time I see him but the way he acts with me. It's more like he's fully invested, not holding large parts of himself back the way he was before.

He's no longer a stranger, and he's even more than a friend. I see him every morning in the breakfast room, and I see him in passing throughout the day. We have the normal counseling appointments, and we also have outings with Fred to the vet and to the groomer and to the pet store to buy him a carload of supplies and toys and a great big luxurious dog bed.

Every day we have dinner and spend the evening together, taking a walk or watching a movie or going for a ride or simply talking.

Our evenings together are starting to feel like dates. They generate the same giddy anticipation and the same fluttery responses.

I can't help but wonder if he feels the same.

On the following Friday, he's not up before me, drinking coffee and reading the newspaper in the breakfast room like normal. I linger even after I finish my bagel, thinking maybe he just slept in.

He doesn't make an appearance, and eventually it's eight o'clock, which is my self-imposed starting time for work. Fred has been sitting in hopeful attention beside the table, and he follows me to the library when I go.

I've been feeling good enough to work full days this past week, and I'm getting into the rhythm of assessing, evaluating, and cataloging book after book, sometimes finding the work engaging and sometimes tedious, which is my impression of almost every job on earth.

I keep waiting for Arthur to make an appearance. He usually stops by the library at least a couple of times a day to see how things are going and what I'm working on.

But not today. I don't see him at all, and the door to his home office whenever I walk by is closed.

Something is off. Maybe something is wrong. This isn't like him at all.

I chat with Stella on and off, but she offers no explanation. I don't ask directly, weirdly shy about admitting I want to know.

By the afternoon, I'm anxious and restless. What the hell is going on?

At five, I save my work and clear my desk, then get up and march to Arthur's office door, Fred at my heels.

This is ridiculous. I'm going to knock. If something is wrong with him, I need to know what it is.

I've raised my hand to rap on the door when I hear his voice, slightly muffled by distance, coming from the entry hall.

Fred gives a happy yap at the familiar voice. He and I hurry toward the sound, bursting out from the hallway to see him standing near the front door.

His hair is pulled back, and he's wearing a dark gray suit with a white shirt and a blue-and-silver tie. He's set a briefcase on the floor next to where he's standing, and he's talking to Stella.

He looks tired. Very tired. As tired as I can ever remember seeing him.

At my arrival, he glances over. His face softens into a smile.

I stand perfectly still, rattled and disoriented and deeply touched by that particular smile. It's like seeing me is the best thing to happen to him all day.

Stella's eyes move between him and me. Her eyes glint with what might be hidden laughter. "Dinner will be ready around seven," she says. "Let me know if you need anything before then."

"Thanks for everything, Stella," Arthur says, his eyes

not leaving my face even as he leans over to pet Fred, who has run over eagerly for his greeting.

When Arthur straightens up, I manage to step over so I'm standing right next to him. "There you are."

His forehead wrinkles. "What do you mean?"

"I mean I didn't know where you were all day. I didn't know you were gone."

"Of course I was gone. What did you think? That I was hiding away in my office or bedroom all day without saying a word to you?" He sounds almost offended.

"N-no."

He moves slightly closer, tilting my chin up so he can see my face better. "You did think that."

"Well, I didn't know. You didn't tell me you were leaving."

"Oh." That appears to stump him.

It gives me an advantage, so I pursue it. "It seems like common courtesy to tell me where you were going and how long you'd be gone so I wouldn't spend the whole day wondering if something was wrong or if you were avoiding me."

His mouth opens. His hand is still gently holding my face. "You were worried?" He sounds utterly stunned.

"Of course I was worried! I'm used to you being around and you weren't. All day you weren't here."

The surprise in his expression is transforming to something resembling gratification. "You missed me." This comment is more a statement than a question.

"Yes, I missed you. Not that you deserve it." I sound and feel a bit huffy. "What's the deal with taking off at the crack of dawn without even a word about being gone?"

He starts to say something, then appears to rethink and says very softly, "I'm not used to anyone caring about my comings and goings."

"Well, I care. So next time tell me if you're leaving."

That fond look is softening his face again, even more obviously than before. It means something to him. That I care about whether he's here or not. "Okay." He's moved his hand so that it's cupping my cheek, but he seems to realize what he's doing just then and drops it. "I will."

"Good." My cheek feels cold and empty without his hand. "So where were you?"

"I had some meetings in DC, and they ended up lasting all day." He shifts his weight, looking briefly uncomfortable.

"Oh. What meetings?"

He darts me a little glance. "Work stuff."

"Oh." I want to know more. I want to know some specifics about what he does all day and what he did today in particular. But he's never volunteered any information about his work, so maybe he doesn't want to share all that with me.

He leans over to pick up his briefcase and gasps, jerking visibly as he straightens up.

"What's the matter?" I ask, reaching out for him urgently since he's obviously in pain.

"Nothing," he mutters, taking a couple of long breaths as he purposefully relaxes his posture.

"Something is wrong. What is it? Is your back acting up again?" My eyes are wide, and I'm thinking of nothing but concern for him.

His gaze shoots over to me. "My back?"

"Y-yeah." His response is confusing. "Don't you... Don't you have a bad back?"

I suddenly realize I have no way of knowing that at all. He's never mentioned it in my conscious memory. He's never acted before like he had any back pain.

"Do you remember something?" He's turned to face me and taken my shoulders in both his hands. His grip is firm but not hard. "Has something come back to you?"

"I don't... I don't know." I'm trying to make sense of the tangle of my mind, but I can't remember any specifics. Nothing except scattered images and feelings that are completely out of context.

I definitely don't remember anything about his back.

But there must be something there given his questioning right now.

"I'm sorry," I say. "It's all a big mess in my mind."

He's already pulling back, reining in his urgency.

"Okay. Then don't worry about it. Maybe more is coming back but you're not even aware of it."

"That could be. I can try to focus more and make myself rem—"

"No! Don't you dare. Don't do anything of the kind." He sounds almost stern.

Ridiculously, it gives me a hot flash of desire. I flush and duck my head.

"The doctor said not to force it. You've been doing well. I'm not going to let you hurt yourself by forcing it before you're ready."

"Okay." I gulp and tell myself that clawing off his suit and running my hands all over his body is a completely inappropriate response to this situation.

"I'm sorry," he says in his normal, gentler voice. He brushes my hair back because I'm hiding behind it. "I didn't intend to sound mean."

"I know you weren't being mean."

"I worry you'll push too hard and do more damage." He tilts my head up, brushing his knuckles over my cheek. "You're doing so good, Scarlett. Try to be patient and let the rest come."

My knees almost buckle. I'm washed with waves of hot desire, and I have no idea why or where they've come from. It's far too embarrassing to let him see—why would I be turned on when he's so sober and concerned about me? —so I close my eyes and breathe deeply.

"That's right," he murmurs, sliding his hand down to span one side of my neck. "Try to relax. Good girl."

God help me. That only made it worse.

"Are you okay?" he asks after a minute.

I've barely gotten myself under control now. I manage to open my eyes and give him a smile. "Yeah. It's just hard being patient."

"That I know." He glances at his hand, gives a little jerk, and lets go of me like he's been burned. The move evidently jars his back again. He winces.

"You're back *is* bad!" The concern effectively distracts me from my arousal. "I knew it was hurting. Please say it isn't from carrying me to bed the other night."

"No. It wasn't from that. It's from sitting tensely in uncomfortable chairs all day. It'll be fine." He stretches his spine, making another face that proves his discomfort.

"What do you normally do when it gets bad?"

"Ignore it," he admits.

"Arthur."

"I usually take a hot shower. That sometimes helps."

"Okay, good. Then that's what you should do now." I take his arm and make him walk with me down the hall and to the stairs. We head up slowly. He's obviously in more pain than he wants me to see. When we get to his room, I push into the bathroom and turn on the shower, making sure the water is hot.

He stands in the doorway, watching me bemusedly.

"What?" I ask, suddenly self-conscious. It's hardly my job to do all this for him. "I was just making sure you're actually going to take the shower."

"I will." He starts loosening his tie, then slides off his suit jacket.

I want to help him. I want to take off all his clothes. But that's hardly appropriate. "Okay. I'll let you get in. Take a long one and try to stretch out your back. I'll come check on you after a while."

"You don't have to—"

"I'll be back to check on you." I make my voice as firm as possible, and then I make myself leave the bathroom.

I go to my room and, restless and flustered, end up taking a quick shower myself. I feel better when I get out, and I take more time picking out my clothes than normal as I re-dress.

I want to look pretty, but I don't want to look like I'm trying too hard. So I pick out a pair of soft gray lounge pants and a loose rose-colored top that looks good with my skin and accentuates my curves.

It's a comfortable, cozy outfit. Not a date outfit. Surely Arthur won't think there's anything strange about it.

I take Fred outside, and Billy wants to take him on a walk, so I head back inside alone.

When I reach Arthur's room, I knock on the door. I left it open just a crack, but it doesn't seem polite to just barge in.

For a moment, as my knuckles hit the door, I have the strongest sense of déjà vu. A flash of Arthur naked in the shower, his back to me, his ass muscles clenching.

What the hell?

"Come in," he calls, sounding a bit startled.

"It's just me." I force the hot visual out of my mind and swing the door open.

To my surprise, Arthur was lying on the bed—on top of the duvet. He's in the process of sitting up, but he can't do it quickly.

There's no mistaking the twisting on his face.

"Damn it, Arthur. Don't get up." I stride over to the bed in an attempt to stop him from standing. "Lie back down. Is it really bad?"

"It's fine." He sounds out of breath, and he doesn't argue about reclining again. That alone is proof his back is really bothering him.

"Didn't the shower help?" I know he took one. He smells like soap, and his hairline is damp.

"It did." He's got his head on the pillow now, his eyes focused on the ceiling. I suddenly wonder if he's embarrassed. "It's really fine. It's been a lot worse than this before. A couple of times I couldn't even get out of bed."

"Well, you need to take care of it now so it doesn't get that bad again. What would help?"

"I just need to stretch it out, I think. I'll be fine in a few minutes." He slants his eyes over toward me. "It's really not an emergency. I must have gone too long today without giving it a break. If I'm careful, it'll be better tomorrow."

"Then tomorrow you need to take it easy."

"I will."

"I mean it."

His mouth softens. "I will. I promise."

"What can I do now? Do you need an ice pack or something to put on it?"

"No. I just need to let the muscles relax, and then I'll be fine."

"Oh well, that's easy then. Roll over."

He blinks. "What?"

"Roll over."

"Why?"

"I'm going to give you a back rub."

"I don't need—"

"You said your muscles need to relax. I can help with that. So stop being a stubborn toddler about it and roll over."

He looks at me for several seconds, and I'm honestly not sure what he'll do. He's not the type of man who's used to being vulnerable in any way. But then he relents. Slowly turns himself over so he's lying on his stomach.

"Getting kind of bossy, aren't you?" he mutters.

I snort. "Maybe I've always been bossy and you never knew. Are you okay in this position?"

"Yeah. I'm fine. You really don't have to do this."

"I know I don't have to. I want to help, and this is the only thing I can think of. I'm not an expert at massage or anything, so let me know if something doesn't feel good or makes your back worse."

He makes a throaty sound that doesn't form a real word.

"You have to tell me, Arthur."

"I will," he says hoarsely. Then "Thanks."

I've been so concerned about his well-being that I'm only now really noticing that he didn't put a shirt on when he got out of the shower. He's wearing nothing but the old gray sweats he wore last week.

His skin is firm, stretched smoothly over long bones and natural muscle development. His sweats are low on his hips. I can see the top of his butt, and it makes me want to gulp.

I run my hands up and down the length of his back. Hear him take a quick breath.

"Is it your lower back?"

"Yeah."

I press a little firmer, rubbing from his shoulders down to the small of his back. I could really use some lotion, but looking for some feels like a hassle, so I do my best without it. His breath hitches again when I move lower. The muscles are very tight. No wonder he's sore.

"You're way too tense. You should get professional massages."

"It never seemed worth the trouble. I'm really fine without—"

"Stop trying to get me to give up. I really don't mind. I want to help."

I rub down the lines of his muscles, finding the hard little trigger points and pushing into them. He inhales sharply and exhales thickly. The sounds make my belly clench.

This isn't sexy, but it's intimate. The coiled feeling inside isn't arousal, but it's akin to it—like he's mine and it's my job to take care of him.

To distract myself from that direction of thoughts, I ask, "So what meetings did you have today?"

"Work stuff," he mumbles. His head is turned to the side, his eyes closed.

"I know it's work stuff. I was wondering what work stuff. What kind of meetings did you have? Don't you normally do your work remotely?"

"Yeah. This was different. I'm working on some reorganization that we were finalizing, and it was easier to be there in person."

"What kind of reorganization?" I've moved my hands up and down his back and located where the muscles are tensest, where the worst trigger points are. I start focusing there, applying more pressure.

He releases a groan as I push down on his lower back.

"Is that too much?" I ask, lightening the pressure immediately.

"No," he rasps. "It's good." He shifts his legs slightly.

"What kind of reorganization?"

He doesn't answer immediately, so I wait. Then he finally says, "I'm changing the leadership structure for a lot of the Worthing holdings."

Genuinely interested, I ask, "In what way?"

"So I'm not the final decision-maker for everything."

"Oh my goodness. That's a major change, isn't it?"

"Yeah. Generations of my ancestors may rise up and strike me down any day now."

"Well, let them. Who cares about them? I think it's a good idea. It will take a lot of pressure off you, won't it?"

"Yeah."

"Good. Are you just trying to lighten your load, or are you taking all that stuff off your plate completely?"

"Not completely but most of it. I..." He gasps when I start pressing into a different spot. "Oh fuck."

I lift my hands. "I'm sorry. Was it hurting?"

"No. Please don't stop."

Flushing and feeling quite fluttery, I get back to work. He lets out another one of those soft moans that make me clench.

When I find my voice, I prompt, "You were telling me you were taking most of the Worthing stuff off your plate."

"Yeah. I'm transferring a lot to my cousins, and I've got a couple of other good people who are going to take the reins on some of it. I never wanted to do it—manage so many different streams of business."

"You should have told your dad no."

"Mm-hmm."

"Not that I'm one to talk. I know how hard that is to do. I'm really glad you're doing it now. What are you going to do with your time afterward?"

"I haven't decided yet. I've thought…" He clears this throat. "I was thinking about graduate school."

"That would be amazing!" I'm so excited I stop massaging him momentarily. "You should definitely do that. You could get your PhD and teach. You'd be the world's best professor."

He chuckles at that. He sounds almost relieved. I have no idea why.

"Well, now that you're reorganizing, you'll have the chance to rest more and take it easier on your back."

"If you say so."

"I do say so. I'm serious. It's only going to get worse if you're not careful. Don't do any work this weekend."

"Okay. I won't."

Pleased and excited about the idea of his new career path, I have to force myself to pay attention to my hands. I want to pet him, but that's not what he needs. He needs to unclench some of these muscles.

As my massage becomes more intense, his vocal responses become more uninhibited. He moans, long and hoarse and satisfied, and he mutters out breathless curses. Mostly "Oh fuck."

My work is effective. I can feel his body softening beneath my hands. I move lower down his body so I can push into his butt through the fabric of his sweats.

"Fuck, baby," he mumbles. "So good. You're so good."

The coiled pressure of complex feelings below my belly throbs with sudden, intense arousal. I slide my hands back to his back, finding another spot to focus on.

I work on him for more than half an hour, until he's relaxed and boneless and still moaning softly. If I go any farther, I'll start touching him in less appropriate ways.

I'm pleased and proud and tender and still a little aroused when I finally pull my hands away. "Okay. I hope that helped."

"*Helped* doesn't even come close to how good that was. Thank you, Scarlett."

I blush at the compliment. "You're welcome."

I wait for him to get up, but he doesn't.

"Are you all right?" I ask after a minute.

"Y-yeah."

"It doesn't sound like you're all right. What's wrong?"

"Nothing's wrong."

"Did I make your back worse?"

"Of course not." He sounds more like himself now. Clever and faintly wry. I certainly don't expect him to admit, "I'm in a condition that's going to make you uncomfortable, so you might want to leave before I get up."

I'm flustered, so I don't immediately understand what he means. Then... "Oh."

"It's not a big deal."

It feels like a big deal. He's aroused. He has to be. Turned on. By my back rub. "I'm sorry. I didn't mean to—"

He sits up with a groan. Straightens up on the edge of the bed, then pulls me over so I'm facing him. "You didn't do anything, Scarlett."

My eyes dart down to his lap. He's definitely turned on. I can see the shape of his erection beneath the thin cotton of his pants.

"You didn't do that. You were being kind and generous. It's not your fault I got turned on. The state of my body is my responsibility. Not yours. And don't ever let a man tell you differently."

I swallow hard, my skin hot but my heart fluttering wildly.

"Do you understand?"

"Yes." I lick my lips. "Was it just... being touched? Or was it... Was it...?"

"It was being touched by you," he admits, sober and gentle. "But I don't want you to stress about it. You have enough to deal with right now with losing your memory. You don't also need to be burdened with the weight of all my needs. I'm not going to let you be dragged down by that."

"I don't... I don't feel dragged down."

If anything, I feel like I want to fly.

"Okay. Good." He glances down at himself. "So don't worry about this. Thank you for the back rub. It really did help."

"Okay. Good." I realize I'm repeating what he said. I can't seem to think of new words.

I want him to kiss me. To take me in his arms. To murmur out all kinds of stern, hot commands and encouragements. To fuck me with that erection.

But things aren't like that between us. He's made it very clear—no matter what his body feels—the rest of him isn't going to do that.

So I can't push. He's probably right. I might not be in a fit state to judge what I want. There's too much confusion in my mind. I can't even sort out what's a dream and what's not.

"Are you okay?" he murmurs. His hands are still on my hips as I stand between his parted legs.

"Yeah. I'm okay."

"Good. I need some time alone, but I'll see you at dinner."

"Okay. That sounds good." I don't want to leave him, but he's making it clear it's not a rejection.

"Thank you, baby."

"You're welcome." I turn to leave, smiling to myself at the endearment. He called me baby twice this afternoon.

I knew I wasn't imagining it last week when he carried me up to bed.

10

THE FOLLOWING FRIDAY, ARTHUR, FRED, AND I GO ON A HIKE.

The idea and plan is formed so spontaneously I can barely keep up. When I walk into the breakfast room at just after seven with Fred at my heels, Arthur is drinking coffee like normal. His eyes smile over the top of his newspaper as he says good morning.

I make a friendly comment about how nice the day is —crisp and sunny and not too warm, the perfect day for a walk—and before I know it, Arthur suggests that's what we should do and that's exactly what's happening.

Stella prepares us a picnic, we gather a few supplies,

and then Arthur and I settle Fred into the back seat of the SUV and drive forty-five minutes to the parking area for popular hiking trails through scenic hills.

I'm thrilled by the surprise outing. In truth, I feel obliged to check a couple of times to make sure Arthur isn't missing out on important work, but he reassures me he had very little on his schedule today anyway and nothing that couldn't be pushed out to next week.

So I'm able to enjoy the drive and the hike without guilt. We laugh and talk and admire the scenery and watch Fred's ecstatic antics.

Arthur must have already had our destination spot in mind because he directs us to it. The hike there takes about an hour and a half. It's a shaded clearing far enough off the trail to not be seen by passersby with a view of the expansive vista and not far from a creek cascading down a rocky hill.

I'm utterly charmed by the setting, so much so I can't stop oohing and aahing. Arthur appears pleased with my appreciation as he spreads out the blanket we folded and stowed in my backpack.

Arthur was carrying the picnic in his big backpack. It's still a bit early for lunch, but the exercise and fresh air made us hungry, so we eat our sandwiches, pasta salad, grapes, and cookies right away.

Fred begs for food and then investigates the creek,

jumping back dramatically when a frog hops right under his nose.

It's all perfect. I have such a good time I can't stop giggling.

Every time I glance over, Arthur is watching me—either openly or discreetly—with a soft, warm gaze that makes me flutter.

We talk about everything from books to our school years to the lifespan of a grasshopper. Eventually we both stretch out on the blanket, and I'm so relaxed and comfortable I actually doze off.

It's only for about twenty minutes. I open my eyes to find Arthur stretched out on his side right next to me, his eyes on my face.

I smile instinctively because I like the sight of him so much. "Where's Fred?"

"He decided to take a nap too." Arthur nods in the direction of the creek.

I lift my head to see Fred stretched out on his side in the grass not far from our feet. I giggle and lay my head back down, staring up at the sky through the canopy of leaves and branches. "I like it here."

"Me too."

I slant a glance back over at him. "Do you come here a lot?"

"Occasionally. Not for a long while."

"Why not?"

He half shrugs.

"Why not?"

He works his mouth, visibly hesitating before he admits, "Because I've spent years cutting myself off from the parts of life I really want—even simple things like this."

"Oh, Arthur," I breathe, rolling onto my side to face him and reaching out to stroke his cheek and jaw.

"I'm not feeling sorry for myself. I was wrong to do that. I can see it now, but back then it felt... inevitable. Like I didn't have much choice. But I am trying to do better now. That's one of the reasons I'm reorganizing the Worthing holdings. I want to..." He trails off with an uneven exhale, like he's silently laughing at himself.

"What do you want to do?"

"I want to *live*. Someone not long ago told me I should."

I smile because his resolve sounds right, sounds like genuine emotional progress. But there's also a flicker of discomfort at the idea of someone else giving him advice like that. Who was he talking to? And does he trust that person more than he trusts me?

It's jealousy, I realize. I don't want anyone else to hold that intimate place in his life.

"Is something wrong?" he asks, always so observant he can see the smallest shift in my expression.

"No. Nothing at all." My hand is still on his face. I can't

pull it back. "You *should* live. You should do the things you want to do instead of holding back because you feel like you don't deserve them or are trapped by your past and your family. You should *live*, Arthur."

"I'm trying." He tilts his head slightly, leaning into my palm.

I move my fingers until they're tracing the line of his scar. I barely notice it anymore. It's just another feature on his rough, striking face. "Can I ask you something?"

"Anything." He's very still. Almost like he's holding his breath.

"How did you get this scar?"

His lips part, but no sound comes out.

"My dad said you'd never tell anyone."

"He was right."

"Oh. Well, if it's too private, you don't have to tell me." I'm still kind of petting his face. I can't seem to stop myself.

"I want to tell you. I've just never told anyone before. It's... hard." He takes a deep breath. Purposefully relaxes his face and shoulders. Reaches over and takes my free hand in his.

I squeeze his hand.

"How much do you remember of what I've told you about my dad?"

"He was mean and cold. Sometimes hit you when he drank. Very controlling. More interested in the Worthing name than he was about you as a person."

"Yes. That's all true. After my mom died, he got worse. I didn't have anyone then, and I wanted his approval more than anything, so I kept trying to please him. When I was thirteen, I told him I wanted to be more involved in Worthing business, and he gave me a work project to do. I was way too young to do it, but I didn't care. I was so proud of the responsibility. I worked for hours every day on it and was sure I'd done a great job."

"I'm sure you did."

"Looking back, I can honestly say it was impressive work for a thirteen-year-old. But it wasn't perfect. And my dad..." He gives a bitter, breathy laugh. "My dad pointed out every single flaw."

"Oh no. I'm so sorry, Arthur." I comb my fingers through his hair, pulling some of it loose from the ponytail in the process.

"It's ages ago now. But I can still remember how much it hurt. Anyway, I wasn't just heartbroken. I was angry at his rejection. I'd spent most of my life avoiding any sort of conflict with him because of how he always exploded, but I was so mad I finally went to confront him late that night."

I'm almost shaking now, so worried about what I'm about to hear.

His tone is quiet, almost delicate, as if he's taking care with every syllable. "He'd been drinking. If I'd known, I probably would have changed my mind since he was always at his worst when he drank, but I didn't know. I went to his office and demanded he talk to me and then let him have it about how bad a father he was and how I deserved more."

"You were right in what you told him. You did deserve better. And you were trying to stand up for yourself."

"I was. For the first time in my life."

"What did he do?"

"He was so angry. He roared at me, told me to get out. I didn't immediately, and he... He pushed me."

I suck in a breath although I'd known it had to be something like that.

"I fell against a table with an antique vase on it, and then it fell with me to the floor. It shattered, and I landed badly on a piece of it." He rubs a finger up and down his scar. "So I ended up with this."

"I thought maybe he cut you on purpose."

"No. His violence was always in an explosion of anger. He never did it in a calculated way. Not that it makes it any better." He gives another of those bitter chuckles. "He always prided himself on being so controlled."

"He was terrible."

"Yes. He was."

"I'm glad you're finally making your own decisions instead of letting him control you from the grave. You aren't what he made you."

His expression softens. "I'm partly what he made me, but there's more to me than that."

"Exactly. It's the same with me and my dad. I'm partly what he made me. So desperate to be loved that I bury my own needs to please other people. But I'm more than that too. I'm trying to do better, just like you."

"You *are* doing better." He slides one hand around to the back of my neck, under my hair. "You are so amazing. To have lived through what you've lived through and still be so kind and generous and resilient and softhearted."

"I feel the same way about you." It feels like my heart may fly all the way out of my chest now.

"Do you?" He seems to be asking more than what's on the surface. He's suddenly urgent. Almost hungry.

"Yes, Arthur. I really do." I scoot closer to him, holding on to his ponytail.

He makes a little moan and closes the gap between our mouths, kissing me deep and slow.

It feels so good I respond eagerly, and my enthusiasm soon transforms the gentle kiss to something a lot deeper.

Soon he's got me rolled over on my back with him on top of me. He's parted my thighs to make room for his body, and I've bent one of my knees and wrapped a leg around his hip. I'm grinding against his groin as his tongue thrusts rhythmically into my mouth.

"Oh fuck, baby." He lifts his head to gaze down at me. His face is flushed, and his eyes have darkened. "Look at you. So hot and eager. And I've barely started touching you."

I claw my fingernails down the back of his shirt, hating so many layers between us. "Arthur, please."

He moans again before he leans into another kiss. This time his hand slides between my legs, rubbing me there over my jeans.

I whimper and arch, utterly shameless in the face of the desire flooding my body.

But then he yanks his mouth away with an agonized groan, holding himself up on straightened arms above me. "Hold on a minute."

"I don't want to hold on."

"Me either. But we need to think. I don't want to do this without thinking and then have you regret it."

"I'm not going to—"

"I don't have protection."

"Oh." I blink, the urgency of my desire taking a sudden nosedive at unavoidable realities.

"We could throw caution to the wind and do it anyway. But we might have to live with the consequences. And I'm still worried about you moving too fast before you've fully recovered. Can we take a little time and then decide?"

I've breathed deeply enough to calm the worst of my arousal. I'm still uncomfortable but not on the edge of frantic. I know he's right. I might not like it, but I know he's right. "A little time? So you're not saying no for good?"

"Fuck no." He finally sits up, shaking himself off with a little groan. "I'm clearheaded about wanting you, Scarlett.

And if you can tell me you've thought about it and come to a conscious decision rather than giving in to physical desire, then I'm all in."

I understand what he's saying. This isn't a rejection at all. My mind has been muddled lately. He didn't say so, but we both know it's true. He wants me to want this for real.

And that's what I want too.

"Okay." I sit up too, part of me relieved from the reprieve from a life-changing decision. "That makes sense. We shouldn't have sex without protection since I'm not on birth control. There were some pills in my stuff, but I haven't been taking them since I got back from the hospital. And the last thing I need to deal with right now is an unplanned pregnancy. So we need to at least get home. I can think it through then and make sure this is what I want."

"That sounds good. This evening, after we're home and you've had the time you need, you can let me know if this is still what you want."

"Okay. I will."

Despite the tense interlude, the hike back is fun and companionable. I have just as good a time with Arthur as I did before our little roll on the blanket.

The drive is quiet but in a friendly, comfortable way. We listen to music and occasionally sing to the best songs.

At home, I feed Fred and then leave him with Billy, who has decided the dog is his soulmate and missed him for most of the day.

Then I go take a shower, keeping my hair out of the water so it doesn't get wet. Afterward, I rub myself with spicy-scented lotion, brush out my hair, and put on a little satin robe, tying it closed over my otherwise naked body.

There.

I made my decision back up on the hiking trail. I'm as clearheaded about what I want as I've ever been in my life.

So I walk down the hall and knock loudly on Arthur's bedroom door.

"Hold on," he calls out immediately. It takes a minute or two for the door to swing open.

I stare across the threshold at his mostly naked body, still damp from a shower, covered with nothing more than a towel secured around his waist.

"Is everything all right?" he asks, sounding genuinely worried.

I frown. "Yes, it's all right. I thought we agreed I'd let you know after I thought things through."

His eyes widen. "Already? I wasn't expecting anything until the evening."

I redden with a hot wave of embarrassment. "Oh." I

turn quickly, deciding the best option here is to make an escape. "I misunderstood."

I'm about to start running, but he grabs me before my first step. He turns me back around to face him and then hauls me into his room. "You didn't misunderstand anything."

"You were thinking this evening and I show up at your door about five minutes after—"

"You think I'm disappointed or annoyed? Seriously, Scarlett? Look at me."

My vision clears enough to focus on his face. His eyes have darkened the way they do when he gets excited, and his expression is hungry. Needy.

Thrilled.

There's no possible way to see this man as disappointed.

"Oh."

He chuckles and takes my face in both his hands in that entitled way he's done before. "To tell you the truth, I was talking myself down. Telling myself you'd probably change your mind once you thought things through. So I might have been surprised no matter when you showed up. I... I still don't expect good things to happen to me."

"Well, they can." I'm happy again. Excited. And touched by what he just admitted. "There's no reason you shouldn't be happy."

"You're sure about this? No doubts or confusion? This is what you really want, and you want it right now?"

"Yes. This is what I want. And I want it right now." I'm beaming up at him, which is probably not the sexiest expression ever, but I can't seem to manage anything else at the moment.

His eyes blaze. Joy more than lust. "You already know I want this too."

I do. Somehow that truth has settled into my heart, more quickly and naturally than I would have expected. He wants me—and he wants more than just my body.

I know it for sure.

"So we can do this now then?" I ask.

He doesn't answer with words. He leans down, holding my head in place with his hands so he can claim my lips. The kiss deepens even quicker than before, and soon he's got me backed up against the wall next to the still-open bedroom door.

I arch eagerly against the wall as I clutch at his neck and then slide my hands down his bare back. His tongue is doing that sensual thrusting again, and it's really turning me on.

Without ever breaking the kiss, he reaches over to close the bedroom door and then turns the lock. I whimper into his mouth and try to wrap a leg around his thighs, desperately needing some friction at my center.

After a few minutes, he kisses his way down to my

neck, sucking my pulse point and then moving up to scatter kisses along my jaw and cheeks.

I moan, almost losing my balance at the pleasure of it.

"You're so beautiful," he mumbles against my skin. "So sweet. Tell me you want this."

"I want this." I gasp when one of his hands slides down to cup my bottom over the silky robe. "I want it so bad."

He straightens up, giving my mouth a soft, quick kiss. "Tell me if there's anything we do that you don't like."

"I will."

"Okay, good." He's breathing fast already. His hair is wet from the shower and hasn't been pulled back, so it's hanging wetly around his face and shoulders. His tone is still soft but not quite as gentle as he adds, "Then turn around."

The flood of hot desire prompted by his words is like nothing I've ever experienced. I gasp and start to tremble.

He waits and watches until I can make myself move. I slowly turn my back to him so I'm facing the wall.

He reaches around to untie the sash to my robe. It falls open. I gulp at the cool air of the room against my newly bared skin.

He kisses the back of my neck and then slides the fabric of my robe down to expose my shoulders and runs kisses back and forth across both of them. In the process, he raises one of my hands and then the other and plants them against the wall.

I stay where he puts me, already so aroused I can barely stand still.

He turns my head so he can kiss me over my shoulder. I whimper into the kiss, throbbing and tingling from my feet all the way up to my head. "You're doing so good, baby," he murmurs thickly when he breaks the kiss. "Do you like it like this?"

"Yeah." I sound stretched, girlish. "Yeah, I like it so much."

"Okay. Try to hold this position no matter how good you start to feel."

"I will."

I have no idea how he instinctively knew so clearly what turns me on the most, but I'm thrilled that I don't have to try to tell him and that he seems to want it like this too. He's such a gentle man at heart I wouldn't have expected him to want to take control like this, but it's clear he does.

And I've never felt more free.

I push against the wall, making another mewling sound as he kisses the back of my neck again and reaches around with one hand to fondle my naked breasts. He tweaks my nipples, each time causing pleasure to tug sharply between my legs.

It's so torturously good I can't help but squirm and gasp.

"Shh." He softens his hands on my breasts and mouths

the side of my throat. "You're so good, baby. Let yourself feel this good. I'm giving it to you. You're allowed to accept it. Don't try to fight it."

I make a weird sobbing sound as my body goes still.

"That's right. Perfect. Just like that." He moves one of my hands and slides off the sleeve of the robe, then repeats the process with the second sleeve until the robe has fallen in a puddle at my feet.

I'm completely naked now, standing with my arms braced against the wall.

"Beautiful." He gently adjusts my stance so my legs are parted more widely.

I whimper as I feel a trickle of moisture on my inner thigh.

He starts working on my breasts again—this time with both hands. I channel the aching need into the loud moans I'm making and manage not to move my hands or hips.

He keeps murmuring out soft encouragements, making the whole thing even hotter. Finally he says against my ear, "Now tell me what you need."

"I need to come. Please, Arthur."

He moves a hand between my legs, feeling me there and then sliding two fingers inside me. "Like this?"

"Yes. Just like that. I need it."

He pumps his fingers slow and steady. I can't help but

arch my spine and lift my bottom, pushing back against his hand.

"That's so good, baby. Let yourself feel it. Don't hold anything back."

There's no way I can stop myself now. I'm already halfway to orgasm, and the pressure intensifies as he accelerates his rhythm and fucks me hard with his fingers.

I cry out loudly as the orgasm breaks and keep grunting as he builds me back up to another. After the spasms finally fade, he pulls his fingers out from inside me, turns me around, and kisses me hard.

I surrender to the kiss completely—free and safe and needy and loved all at the exact same time.

I never thought it was possible before.

After a couple of minutes, he walks us over to the bed, still halfway in the kiss. Then he lays me down and moves on top of me, continuing the kiss from the new position. I eagerly pull off the towel from his waist so he's as naked as me.

He's hard. His erection presses against my middle. I reach between our bodies so I can stroke him.

He grunts into the kiss. And then does it again when I apply a little more pressure.

"Arthur," I gasp, turning my head away from his. "I want you inside me. I don't want to wait anymore."

Strong emotion twists on his face. I'm not entirely sure what it is, but it looks almost desperate. "I want that too."

"So we've both waited long enough."

He lets out a long, soft groan, then gives me a quick kiss and reaches for a condom in the drawer of the nightstand. After he rolls it on, he turns me over onto my stomach and lifts my ass before lining himself up behind me.

I didn't even have to ask for it this way. Somehow he already knew.

I turn to watch him over my shoulder, and he leans over to kiss me again right before he eases inside me.

I make a silly, helpless sound. Pleasure, not discomfort. He's big, but I don't feel as tight as I would have expected. He fits inside me exactly right.

He's stifling a lot of groans, and his face is twisting in pleasure as he eyes me hotly from behind. When we've both adjusted to the penetration, he braces himself above me and pumps his hips with a fast, steady rhythm.

I urge him on, pleading for more, faster, harder. I bump my butt back toward his thrusts. He's grunting in a base, primitive way I never would have expected for such a sophisticated man.

He brings me to orgasm—so good I have to sob into the pillow—and then pulls out, turns me over onto my back, and buries himself inside me again, pulling my legs up around his waist.

My whole body shudders with pleasure and release as

he fucks me like that—faster and tighter and less controlled.

"Yes, Arthur!" I dig my fingernails into the clenching flesh of his ass. "Take me like this. Let go. You let go too."

It takes a while for him to release his control enough to reach climax, but when he does, it's breathtaking. Powerful. He lets out a loud, rough exclamation as his face transforms. Then his hips jerk and his body shakes as he rides out the spasms.

He collapses on top of me afterward. I wrap my arms around him. Experiencing his release—how much of himself he poured into it, into me—was just as exhilarating as surrendering to my own release.

I hold him until he's able to lift his head and kiss me tenderly. "Baby" is all he says.

His eyes are saying a lot more.

I smile and brush back his messy hair. "First times are usually kind of awkward, but not this. I can't believe it."

"We're really good together."

"Yes. We are. That was the best sex I've ever had."

He looks briefly surprised. Then gratified. He kisses me again before he admits, "Me too."

We lie in bed together for about an hour, until it's almost time for dinner. So we get up and put on some clothes and pull ourselves together.

I keep slanting him little looks and trying not to giggle. Just an overflow of giddy feeling.

Before we leave the room, he turns me to face him, his expression sobering. "How are you feeling about this?"

"I feel... great."

"Yeah?"

"Yeah. No regrets at all. And I really want to do it again."

"Good. There's no pressure here. I don't want you to get hit with the whole weight of expectations you're not ready for. But I'd like to continue this too."

"That's all right then. It seems like we're on the same page." I beam up at him. "Right?"

He huffs. "Right.

"Good. Then I need to go find Fred before the poor dog thinks I've completely abandoned him."

11

I WAKE UP WHEN THE BED BESIDE ME SHIFTS. I REACH OUT instinctively, fumbling until I feel a warm, firm body.

I smile.

Arthur.

It's been a month since the first time we had sex, and waking up beside him is one of my favorite things.

"What time is it?" I mumble, not quite getting my eyes open yet.

"Almost five. In the afternoon, not the morning."

"Oh yeah. We were taking a nap, weren't we? What were you doing just now?"

"I was in the bathroom. I was trying not to wake you up."

I roll over onto my side and blink my eyes open. He's lying on his side facing me, the covers pushed down to his waist. His hair is loose and messy around his face. He needs to shave, and his eyebrows could really use combing.

He's utterly scrumptious.

"I don't mind being woken if I don't actually have to get up." I stretch under the covers. It's cool in the room but warm in the bed.

He rearranges his body onto his back and pulls me over to his side, his arm around me. I kiss his chest, but it's soft and idle rather than the start of something passionate. We already had sex earlier in the afternoon and took a nap afterward.

Arthur exhales deeply, his body relaxing as if he's enjoying the lazy afternoon too. He likes having sex, but he's in his forties and isn't motivated to jump into bed multiple times a day.

We have sex nearly every day, but it isn't always long, sustained, and creative. Earlier today we were kind of tired so weren't up for anything athletic or adventurous. We kissed for a while and then he rolled me over onto my stomach and lay on top of me, rocking into me from behind with one of his arms around me.

I turned my head so we could keep kissing, and it felt as warm and intimate as missionary ever has.

I fell asleep with his weight halfway on top of me, and it might have been the safest I've ever felt in my life.

He brushes a few kisses into my hair as I snuggle against him now.

He hasn't yet told me he loves me. He hasn't said a word about deeper feelings. He's evidently still committed to taking it day by day and not defining our relationship with words.

That's the only thing that's been bothering me for the past four weeks. Otherwise I might have been perfectly happy.

Because the truth is I want everything from him, and it doesn't feel like I have it yet.

We doze together for about thirty more minutes. Then it feels like his eyes are open, so I tilt my head up to check.

They are. There's a fond, leisurely smile in his eyes but not on his lips as he looks at me.

He's happy like I am. I don't know why he doesn't want to commit to this.

I'm not expecting marriage and babies and a lifetime of domestic bliss. We've only been together a month. But surely it wouldn't be out of the question to acknowledge we're in a real relationship.

"Earlier I was looking at what's left to do in the library,"

I say, light and casual so he doesn't think I'm bringing this up for a significant reason.

"Yeah?"

"Yeah. I'm thinking there's maybe three more months of work to do. I'm more than halfway done."

"That's great."

"I'm not sure what I'll do when I'm done."

He shifts slightly, trying to see me better. "What do you mean?"

"I mean when the library is completed, I'll need to find another job. I'll have to... I don't know... move... or something." I intended the topic to be easy and natural, but I'm stumbling over words, making it awkward.

He's frowning with his mouth and his eyebrows. "With your experience, I'm sure you'll be able to find something. Or I can find you another project around here if you'd rather."

It's a kind thought, but it isn't what I was hoping to hear right now. Surely he knows I was hinting around.

"Are you upset about it?" he asks, cupping my face with his big, warm hand.

I bite my bottom lip. Shake my head and then realize the gesture is a lie. "I'm not really upset. But I don't do well without knowing... without being sure of things. And everything feels so up in the air. It's hard to plan for the future."

He stays still for several seconds, obviously thinking

through what I've said. Then his face twists—like he has something to say—but he reins in whatever strong feeling is prompting it. Says in his gentlest voice, "I know your future is up in the air. I want to help with that as much as you'll allow me. But in terms of us... if part of the uncertainty you're referring to is about that, I'd rather..." He seems to get choked. Has to clear his voice.

"You'd rather what, Arthur?" It feels like I'm holding my breath. Like I'm frozen in bleak anticipation. Like everything is about to change. Like all my dreams are in the balance.

But also like I already know what's about to happen.

"I'd rather we keep things as they are, taking it day by day."

The room and Arthur's face darken before my eyes before they materialize again, sharper and colder than before. My mouth is too dry. I try to moisten it with my tongue. "Okay."

I want to scream at him. Pound on his chest. Demand he tell me why he's still holding back, still won't commit.

But there's only one real answer.

He must not love me enough.

"I know it feels like we could be more than this," he goes on, hoarse and faintly stretched. He's not quite meeting my eyes. "But it's very important to me that there not be any pressure. You've been through a lot. You're still recovering—not just from losing your dad but from what happened before it and from being in that accident. You have your whole life ahead of you, and you've never really had the chance to live it. I don't want you to be cornered into a relationship with me."

That doesn't sound too bad. It gives me an unexpected flicker of hope. "I don't feel cornered. I've never felt that way."

"Good. I'm trying very hard not to do that to you. I need you to be free—to live exactly the life you want."

It's so hard to admit it out loud, but I make myself say it. "But I want... I want *this*. What we have."

His face tightens in something resembling a wince. "And you can have it. For as long as you want."

I stare at him, trying to understand what he's telling me, what's motivating it. "Don't you want—?" My voice breaks. I have to start again. "Don't you want something too?"

"I want what we have, and I want you to be free. That's what I want, Scarlett."

"O-okay."

That's not what I want to say. I want to berate him. Make him tell me everything. Admit he doesn't love me if that's what's prompting his behavior right now.

But if he doesn't want more, he doesn't. Defying it won't change anything.

What the hell else can I say but "okay"?

"Are you all right, baby?"

He sounds so tender. I really don't understand how he can sound so tender and still keep pushing me away.

His tone makes me cry.

"Oh, please don't." He pulls me into a soft hug.

I shake against him, burying my face in his chest.

"I don't want to be free," I finally manage to say.

"You say that now because you've never been free before. But twenty years from now, when you're trapped in a life with an old man, having never had the chance to do the things you want to do, it's going to matter to you. I won't let that happen. I want you in my life for as long as you want it too, but I'm never going to do that to you. I won't."

His words only make it worse. Because he's alluded to the thing I want the most—a life with him—and immediately rejected it as unwanted. I sob against him, held together by nothing but his warm eyes and fast-beating heart.

"O-okay," I mumble again when my crying has finally faded.

"Do you understand?"

"Yes. I understand."

I do. I've heard what he's told me, and I know what it means.

I'm never going to get what I want from him.

He loosens his arms. Lifts his head and peers down at my face. "Are you okay?"

"Yes. I'm okay. I understand."

He doesn't look happy. His face twists like whatever he sees in my expression upsets him. "I'm not saying this has to end. We can still be together—the way we've been this past month. We've been happy, haven't we?"

"Yes." It comes out as almost a croak. "We have."

"So you'll be okay?"

"I'll be okay."

There's nothing else to say. We stare at each other for a couple of minutes. Then he gets out of bed, frowning and thoughtful. "I want you to talk to me, Scarlett. Nothing has to change between us."

"I understand." I'm repeating that too often, but there are no more words for me to say.

I know the situation now—I know everything—and it's never going to be what I want it to be.

"Scarlett."

"I'm okay. Really." I force a smile. "Kind of upset, but I'll be okay."

"Okay." He leans down to kiss me briefly. "I'll give you some space. I'm going to take a shower."

"Sounds like a plan."

He doesn't look happy as he leaves my bedroom. He'll go to his room and take a shower. Get dressed. Wait for me to come out of my room. Then probably try to talk to me again, ease things over, make it better.

The conversation didn't go the way either of us wanted. But the problem is we want entirely different things.

And evidently we always will.

As soon as he closes my bedroom door, I stand up, smoothing down the oversized T-shirt I'm wearing.

I have a choice. A very clear choice. I can go along with what Arthur said, what he wants for the both of us. I can accept it, shape myself around his desires and not mine, and end up never having what I really want.

Or I can do something else. I hear it now in Dr. Walters's voice. *You can accept less than what you want the way you always have, or you can make a difficult choice.*

I stand in the middle of my room, shuddering slightly at how hard this particular choice is going to be.

But I've come a long way from the girl who gave up everything that was hers to do what her father wanted.

I'm not going to give up any more.

Running to the closet, I retrieve an overnight bag and stuff some clothes into it along with my laptop and tablet. Then I put my phone and charger into my purse and throw on jeans with my T-shirt. All that's left is to put on my shoes and sneak out of the house.

I don't have a car. It makes things difficult. I have to walk several blocks to reach a gas station where I get a rideshare.

It's surreal. I'm actually doing this. Leaving without

saying a word to Arthur—or even to Stella and Billy, who have never been anything but warm and kind to me.

But making this choice is the hardest thing in my life, and this is the only way I'll ever get it done.

An hour later, I'm sobbing on the phone with Jenna, trying to explain to her what happened. I had the rideshare drop me at a rental-car place, and I'm now driving a small rental sedan south on the highway.

"Scarlett, I'm so sorry. I can't really understand what you're saying. Do you think you can stop crying enough to explain it? So you just left?"

I sniff and clear my tears enough to see the road. There's not much traffic at the moment, but that could change at any time. And accidents can happen even without other people around. "Yes. I had to get out of there."

"And you rented a car? Are you're driving right now?"

"Yes."

"Well, stop. You're too upset."

"I'm okay."

"Stop saying that. You're not okay. You got your heart broken, and it's terrible. You shouldn't be driving."

"But I want to come see you."

"I want that too, but only when you're in better shape

to drive. Why don't you stop at the first hotel you see and get a room? Spend the night there, and then you can drive down here tomorrow morning."

That's good advice. I know she's right because I can feel tears pooling in my eyes again. I'm exhausted and sad and completely distracted. My father died in a car accident. I'm not going to risk the same thing happening to me.

"Okay. That's a good idea. There will be something coming up at an exit here soon."

"Good. But I still don't understand why you left without saying anything to Arthur."

"He already said what he has to say."

"Maybe. But it doesn't ring true to me."

"It is true! I promise he said it."

"I know he said it. I just don't think he meant it. I don't know him, of course, but you've told me a lot about him in the past four months. He's obviously crazy about you. Why would he still be keeping his distance?"

"He wants me to be free."

"Yeeeaaaaah. I get that. But you can be free and still have him admit that he loves you."

"He doesn't love—"

"Yeah, that's what I don't believe."

Her words are giving me flickers of hope that are far too dangerous to indulge. "Jenna, don't. You're the one who's always saying not to read things into what men say and do. If a man wants to commit, he will. If he's stalling, it's because he doesn't really want to. He's using all these excuses about what's best for me, but if he wanted me for real, he wouldn't be holding back. He *wouldn't*."

"That's normally what I'd assume."

"So this is no different. I've thought about it and relived the conversation over and over again. I think I get it. He's a good guy. He doesn't want to hurt me by rejecting me. So he's manufactured this excuse of what's best for me to give him an out."

"I don't know—"

"I do know. He was acting all kind and gentle and almost... almost paternal. Like he was patting me on the head. That's not a man in love, Jenna. It's not."

"All right."

"You weren't there. You didn't hear him."

"No, I didn't."

"If he doesn't love me, he doesn't love me. But I'm not going to stay there and take scraps instead of getting what I really want."

"That's exactly right. You did good."

I start bawling again out of nowhere. Fortunately, I now spot an interstate sign with three different hotels on it. I take the exit and turn in the direction of the chain I'm most familiar with.

Jenna is still on the line when I park. I've used all the tissues in my purse, so I wipe my face with the damp wad I've collected. "I'm here."

"Okay. Good. See if you can get a room, then call me back."

"Okay." I sniff hard. "I'm sorry I'm such a mess."

"You're not a mess. Don't call yourself that."

"I thought I made so much progress, but here I am again, letting another man drag my feelings around."

"Don't say that," Jenna says sharply. "Don't even think it. It's not true. Look how far you've come. You left even though it was hard. Five months ago, you never would have done that. You'd have stayed and told yourself it was enough and pretended you don't want what you want. Don't you dare question how far you've come. You're making the right decision this time."

So I end up bawling even more.

I've checked in and am walking from the elevator to my room when my phone rings.

I check it, thinking maybe it's Jenna, but it's Arthur's name on the screen.

My throat tightening painfully, I send the call to voice mail, unlock my room, and drop my stuff on the long, low dresser.

I've washed my face, gone to the bathroom, and taken off my shoes when my phone rings again.

Arthur. This time when I reject the call, he leaves a

voice mail. I can't stand the sight of the notification on my phone, so I delete the message without listening.

I can't talk to him right now. If I do, I might cave. I'm stronger than I was, but I'm still not as strong as I should be. If I can't stand my ground, I need to avoid a confrontation.

After a few more minutes, he starts to text me.

Where are you?

Are you all right?

You're scaring me. Please let me know you're okay.

That message really gets to me. It feels like my heart is cracking in my chest. Despite everything, I can't stand the idea of Arthur genuinely scared.

My fingers are shaking as I tap out, *I'm okay. I've left. Please leave me alone.*

The three dots on the screen prove he starts to reply immediately. I wait for his message to appear.

I'm so sorry for everything. I never wanted to hurt you. I was trying to do what was best for you. I never wanted you to leave. Please come back. We can work it out. I know we can.

Then he adds, *If you won't come back, at least tell me where you are so I can come to you.*

He sounds so upset. Almost desperate.

I'm crying again as I block his number and call Jenna back.

Two hours later, I'm lying on my bed, exhausted and dazed and heavy, when a phone rings.

I grab for my cell phone, but that's not where the ringing is from.

It's the landline in my hotel room.

I reach for it automatically. No one but Jenna knows I'm here, so it's got to be the front desk. "Hello?"

"Scarlett, baby, please don't hang up."

I make a choking sound at Arthur's hoarse voice. "I asked you to leave me alone."

"I will. If you need me to, I will. But not without you hearing what I have to say. I can't let you leave like this. Maybe I should. I've been trying so hard to make sure you're perfectly free, that nothing is tying you down. But I can't. I can't! It's too much to ask. I can't be that self-sacrificing. Maybe I'm selfish, but I can't let you go like this. Please talk to me."

I've never heard him like this. Out of control. Babbling. Desperate. It goes right to my heart. My voice wobbles as I say, "You told me what you wanted. It's not what I want. I'm making the best decision for me."

"I didn't tell you what I wanted! I told you what I thought I was supposed to want. You haven't heard the truth from me, baby. Not the whole truth. Please let me tell you the truth now."

I gulp. My mouth goes dry. The room spins briefly before my eyes. "I... Where are you?"

"I'm down in the lobby. They wouldn't give me your room number, but they connected the call to your room."

"How did you know where I was?"

He makes a weird sound in his throat. "I've been making calls since you blocked me. Eventually I landed on the right one."

I clutch at the phone. Make another hard decision. "I'm in room 416. You can come up."

"Thank you, baby."

There's a dial tone immediately afterward. I hang up the phone and then push myself into a sitting position. I rub my eyes and take a few breaths, and I've barely managed to stand up when there's a pounding on the door of my room.

"Hold on," I call. My legs are sore for some reason. I don't know why it's so hard for me to move. Heartbreak shouldn't affect the body this way.

I get to the door, unlock it, and swing it open. Arthur is right there, his hair still half-wet from his shower, loose and drying in wild kinks around his face. He's still unshaven, with shadows under his eyes and an anguished urgency on his face.

His expression cracks when he sees me. "I love you, baby. I love you so much."

I freeze. My mouth drops open. I sway slightly on my feet.

He reaches out and slides an arm around me—support rather than an embrace.

"Wh-what?"

"I love you. I should have told you before. I've felt it for a long time. But I was... I was scared. I told myself I was being selfless and doing the best thing for you, but it was mostly an excuse. I've never been in love before. I've never had anyone love me. It's still hard for me to... to believe this might be real."

"It is real," I whisper, clutching at his shirt as the words wash over me.

"I'm finally... I'm finally recognizing that. Accepting it. That I can love someone and they actually can love me back. But I got scared earlier today when you... when you pressed the issue. I was afraid if I made myself vulnerable, you would... you could reject me. You could break my heart. So I was protecting myself under the guise of protecting you. I'm so sorry. I should have told you the truth."

I could drown in his eyes right now—so warm and soft and deep and tender. "R-really?"

"Yes. When I realized you were gone, it was like my whole world crashed down on me. Everything I almost had was suddenly slipping through my fingers. And there's no way I can let that happen. Not if there's anything I can do to stop it. So this is me. Telling you the absolute truth. Stripping myself naked." He takes a ragged breath and cups my face in both hands. "I love you, Scarlett Kingston. More than I believed myself capable of loving. I'm going to love you all my life. And I do still want you to be free. I want you to be able to make any choices you want for your life even if it means you move and we have to be apart for a while. But I can't just let you go. Not unless you tell me you don't want me."

"I do want you." I can't seem to stop shaking. "I... I love you too."

An awed joy blazes in his eyes, on his face. "Yeah?"

"Yeah. That's why I had to leave. Because I needed more than you were giving me."

"You have it. You have everything. I promise, baby, I'm never letting you go."

Two months later, I'm on my hands and knees on the window seat in the library, and Arthur is fucking me doggie-style, thrusting hard and fast against my ass and murmuring out rough encouragements that intensify my pleasure so much I end up coming over and over.

It lasts a long time, but he finally loses control and comes with a choked exclamation and a look of absolute satisfaction on his face.

We end up tangled together on the window seat, laughing and holding each other.

"You know, I still had a little more work to do today," I say teasingly.

"Then you shouldn't have taunted me that way." He nuzzles my hair. "You knew exactly how I'd react."

I did. Of course I did. He gave me exactly what I wanted.

I beam up at him. "I guess maybe I did."

He chuckles and kisses me softly. "I love you, baby."

"I love you too. And these past two months have been the best of my life."

"Mine too. But you already knew that."

"Can I ask you a question?"

"Of course." He repositions himself, pulling up his underwear and trousers.

"It's not a big deal, but I've been wondering. When did you... when did you start thinking about me differently?"

"To tell you the truth, when you first came here..." He slants me a quick look.

"What? You're not going to admit something creepy, are you?"

He laughs softly. "No. Not at all. In fact the opposite."

"You didn't like me when I first came here?"

"Of course I didn't dislike you. But I didn't really think about you. When you were younger, you never really crossed my mind. When I thought about you, I recognized you were pretty and clever and softhearted, and I wished you weren't under the thumb of your dad, but you didn't matter that much to me."

I can see he's slightly stiff, like he's worried this admission will upset me.

I lean over to kiss his jaw. "I'd much rather hear that than you perving on me when I was like eighteen."

He relaxes and wraps his arms around me. "It wasn't like that at all. Even when you arrived, I felt bad for you, but I didn't... I didn't expect you to mean so much to me. It came on me slowly. The first time I had an inkling there was more to my feelings was that night when we got hot chocolate in the library. And you..."

I reach up and thumb his upper lip, the way I did back then.

"You remember?"

"Of course I remember. That's probably the first time I started thinking about you differently too."

He smiles, and so do I. We likely would have said more, but Stella taps on the library door, which we wisely kept closed, and tells Arthur there's a plumbing issue downstairs.

He gets up to help deal with it, but before he leaves, he leans down and murmurs in my ear, "It might have taken some time to grow and even longer for me to accept as real, but I have no doubts now, and I'm going to love you forever."

"Me too," I tell him as he leaves the room.

He flashes me a smile over his shoulder.

I'm giggling and flushed and giddy as I get back to my work. I've got another hour left to go today, and there's no reason not to do it.

The book I need is on the very top shelf of the north wall. I climb the ladder and reach for it. I've done the same thing with other books dozens of times.

This one is big, and it slips from my hand as I retrieve it, nearly falling on my head. I grab for it quickly but in the process lose my balance on the ladder.

The last thing I remember is a sudden surge of fear as I fall and the book banging onto the floor right beside me.

12

PRESENT

IT'S BEEN A WEEK SINCE WE HAD SEX FOR THE FIRST TIME, and I'm sprawled across Arthur's lap at eight thirty in the morning.

He's sitting up on the bed, leaning against the headrest, and I'm draped over his thighs, completely naked.

He's spanking me.

I'm really not sure how it happened. It started with nothing more than a little teasing about Arthur's gray hair, and now he's got two fingers of one hand inside me as he lightly swats my bottom with the other.

I'm gasping and squirming and making ridiculously helpless sobs of pleasure as I come over and over again.

His thick, gentle murmur is an erotic undercurrent to the rhythmic slapping sound. "You're doing so good, baby. Don't hold anything back. Let yourself feel good. This is what you need. I want to give it to you. I want to give you everything you need."

I sob shamelessly into the mattress, my face and ass both blazing hot and tears and saliva dampening the bedding beneath my face. My whole body shakes as another orgasm breaks through me, my channel spasming hard around his fingers.

He's not thrusting or pumping them. He's holding them still—like he wants to feel how hard I'm coming.

He rubs my butt gently until my clenching fades and I've fallen quiet with nothing more than an occasional whimper. "You did so good. You took that so well. Have you had enough, baby?"

"I... I..."

"Tell me the truth," he murmurs almost sternly.

Oh God. I clench around him excitedly again based on nothing but the tone of his voice.

"It feels like you need even more," he says, a smile in his voice now. "But I need you to tell me in words."

"Please, Arthur." I shift restlessly, trying to raise my bottom higher, toward his hand. "I need more."

"Good girl." He brings his free hand down in a sharp smack, the sting of the impact surging into a wave of pleasure that makes me cry out. "Did you like that?"

"Yes. So much. Again. Please."

He spanks me again. And then again. On the fifth slap, I'm coming hard and messy all around his hand again. This time he spanks me through it, murmuring about how good I am, how hard I'm coming, how I've gone so long not letting myself surrender to this pleasure and how he wants me to always feel this good.

Between his voice and the spanks and the penetration of his long fingers inside me, the orgasm is so long and intense that I'm completely spent afterward. I collapse in a boneless heap across his lap, still moaning shamelessly at how my body feels.

He slides his fingers out from inside me—I've gotten so wet it feels like the moisture is everywhere—and uses both hands to caress my bottom, back, and thighs.

"Thank you," I manage to mumble when I'm finally capable of forming words.

"You're welcome. But you really don't have to thank me. That might have been the hottest moment of my life."

I swivel my head so I can see up at his face. He's flushed and damp with perspiration, and his eyes are filled with that hot, fond satisfaction I always see there after sex. "But you didn't even get your turn."

"Oh yes, I did."

I frown, too groggy to immediately interpret his reply.

"I may have... uh, lost it a bit. I told you it was the hottest moment of my life."

A giggle surprises me. He must have come in his boxers. I manage to sit up and then crawl over so I can wrap my arms around him. He pulls me into his lap, hugging me tightly.

We sit like that for a long time, and I'm not sure I've ever felt safer—more treasured, more loved—in my life.

When he shifts slightly beneath me, I finally pull away and scoot over to get off the bed. I'm still pulsing between my legs with little aftershocks, but the rest of me is tired and sated and a bit sore. Especially my butt.

"You okay?" he asks, eyeing me closely. He's wearing nothing but his underwear, his hair loose and rumpled and thick stubble on his chin.

"Never been better. You didn't hurt your back, did you?"

"No. My back is fine."

"Okay, good." I grin at him, leaning over to give him a kiss. "I'm going to take a shower and get dressed. I guess even after that kind of erotic interlude, we have to eventually get started with the day."

After the exciting morning, the day proceeds as usual—Arthur keeps busy in his office while I work in the library. I'm in the groove of cataloging the books and am moving more quickly than I was a week or two ago. At this pace, there's probably no more than a couple of months left of work to do.

I have no idea what I'll do after I'm done. Yes, I could probably get a position at a library somewhere, but the chances of finding one in this area are slim to none.

I don't want to leave Arthur, but we haven't made any commitments. What we have is good, but it's also new. I can hardly make life decisions based on it.

Plus I still don't have back the memory of the lost six months. Without that, it still feels like I'm living in limbo. If I never get it back, however, I'm going to have to work on establishing a life with those months as a permanent gap.

It's a depressing thought, so I filter it out of my conscious mind, focusing on my work instead.

At lunch, Arthur comes into the library, followed by Stella with a lunch tray. Fred has been lying in his library bed, dozing contentedly, but he jumps up ecstatically at the arrival of two of his very favorite people. So far, everyone he has met has been one of his favorite people. We eat salad and sandwiches in the window seat and chat about the current book I'm working on. When we're done eating, Arthur wraps an arm around me and leans me back to rest on him as he lounges against a large cushion.

It's nice. Intimate. Relaxing. He occasionally brushes a kiss against my hair or strokes my arm or thigh, but he doesn't make any sexual advances.

He just holds me as we take a break. I feel close to him,

and I want to be even closer. If I could, I would crawl right inside his body and settle there.

I snicker at the image, and then I have to explain to Arthur, who is naturally curious about my amusement.

I bumble around, trying to give him an honest answer while not bringing up a topic that's inappropriately pushy for only a week into a relationship.

He smiles like he understands the joke, so I rest my head against him again. After a few minutes, he murmurs, "I do want to say something, Scarlett."

His tone is different. It sounds important. I straighten up and turn to look at his face with wide eyes, my heart suddenly racing.

"I've been trying very hard not to push or pressure you." His expression is sober, so gentle. "But you sounded uncertain just now. Uncertain of how much you can say or ask for. And that's not okay with me."

I frown, momentarily confused.

"I've made mistakes in the past, and I'm not going to make the same ones again. I'm not going to risk losing you because I'm afraid of taking a risk. I don't want you to have any insecurity about my feelings for you. So this is not in any way intended to pressure you or demand you recipro-cate right now. You can take all the time you want. I can be patient. But I'm in love with you, Scarlett."

I suck in a gasp, raising a hand to cover my mouth. My heart is racing even more now but not in fear anymore.

"I love you, and I want us to be more than casual." His voice breaks, and he glances away, then takes a breath and turns back to me. "You don't have to reply. I'm not going to be hurt if you can't return my feelings yet. I just want you to know. You can file it away. So however you feel, whatever you want from me, you won't let uncertainty stop you from doing or saying what's in your heart."

"O-okay." I lick my dry lips and try not to melt away from the overload of warm feelings.

"I've lived my life mostly alone. I've never been in love before. So this is the real thing for me. I'm in this all the way. I'm with you—in whatever way you'll let me be."

I make a choked little sob and throw myself against his chest, filled with absolute certainty that this is where I belong.

Maybe I've always belonged here and never knew it until now.

"So you can make any plans for the future you want. Move back to Charlotte to be closer to Jenna. Get a job halfway around the world. Whatever you want. You need to be free to make your own decisions and do what makes you most happy, and I'm going to love you through every step of it."

I pull away so I can look up into his eyes. Brown and warm and so tender. "I don't want to go anywhere else. Not right now anyway. I want to stay here with you."

"Okay." His face twists very briefly. His voice is barely a

rasp. "If you want to think it through after you've completed this project, we can talk about it then. We'll be able to figure things out. I'll be able to move if there's a job somewhere else you want."

"Really?"

"Of course. Didn't you understand what I was saying? Whatever the next step in my life is, I haven't made definite plans yet. So we can make them together."

"I'd like that." I drop my eyes but feel safe enough to raise them again as I admit softly, "The truth is, I'm pretty sure I'm in love with you too."

We have a few more sappy moments. He's more emotional than I would have expected, but nothing could have made me happier.

When we recover and lounge for a little longer on the window seat together, it's almost one thirty and Arthur has an online meeting scheduled to sort out details of the business reorganization with one of his cousins.

I glance outside to where Billy is playing fetch with Fred after coming to retrieve him with the lunch dishes.

Arthur leans over and says against my ear, "I love you."

There's a crash of joy in my heart, but on its heels something else cracks. Cracks inside my brain. Like a mirror fragmenting around a broken image.

I gasp and wince at a sharp pain in my head. Then I close my eyes and breathe through the resulting dizziness.

"Baby, what is it?" Arthur is trying to lift my head so he can see my face. "What's the matter?"

"I don't know. It's like something hit me. Like déjà vu but a lot more intense." I breathe deeply, trying to clear my mind enough to assess what just happened. "It felt like... It felt like I've lived through that moment before."

"Which one?"

"You behind me, telling me you love me." I squeeze my eyes shut, trying to see it again, match it with the fragmented image in my head. "Shit, it's so weird. I've never felt it so intensely before."

"Have you felt it before? Other times?" He's urgent now, framing my face in his big hands and meeting my eyes demandingly. "Have you been remembering things?"

"I always thought they were just... just dreams. They were always about things I wanted." I can't look him in the eye anymore. It makes my head ache. I pull away and stare at the floor. "Are you saying they're real memories?"

"What are they?"

"Random things. Being close to you. Wiping hot chocolate from your lip. Kissing you. Having... Having..."

I trail off as something obvious—crystal clear—finally sharpens in my brain. "They're real? So we... we were together before? Before I lost my memory?" My heart is sinking into my gut. Everything that was so fluttery just a few minute ago is growing hard and heavy and cold.

A quick peek at his face reveals the truth.

He still looks worried, urgent, so gentle.

But he also looks guilty.

"We were... together?"

He slowly inclines his head.

"We were... in love?"

His jaw works a moment before he admits, "Yes."

"And you... You didn't tell me? You lied—" My voice gets shrill. Breaks a few times. I jerk to my feet and turn so my back is to him. I inhale raggedly, trying to catch my breath.

"Scarlett, please let me explain. Please don't assume the worst."

It takes an inhuman effort to quell the outrage inside me, but I manage to do so enough to turn around and face him again. "Okay. Please explain then."

"We were..." His head jerks away like he's fighting deep emotion. But he controls it quickly. "We were together before. It happened slowly. Over time. It was exactly as I said at the beginning. I felt bad for you, and you didn't have anyone else. I wasn't... I didn't think that way about you at the beginning. But we got to know each other. We got to like each other. And we... We fell in love."

"Was it... Was it like it is between us now?"

"Yes. It grew differently this time, but the way we are together now is the way we were together back then. I thought... I hoped... I wasn't sure if you'd ever remember. I thought I'd lost you. So the fact that we... that it's happened a second time feels like a miracle to me."

I want to reach out for him. Hug the broken ache out of his expression. But he didn't only love me. He lied to me.

"I can understand that. It must have been... horrible for you. I can't even imagine having the person you love wake up, not remembering that you were ever together. But why didn't you just... just tell me?"

"The doctor said not to force it. He said—"

"I know what the doctor said. But this is different. This is snatching away a huge part of my life, stealing it from me."

"You lost it, baby. I didn't steal it. Stealing it would be the last thing I'd ever do."

Surprisingly, I'm not close to tears. I mostly feel cold. Kind of empty.

Frozen.

"Yeah. I get that. But you refused to give it back to me, even just in words." I suddenly remember more—that tense conversation he had with Jenna a couple of days after I came home from the hospital. "Jenna wanted to tell me! You wouldn't let her. She said it wasn't fair to me. She was right. Arthur, how could you have—?"

"I'm so sorry. I had no idea what to do. You were looking at me like a stranger. How could I have told you back then that you'd given your heart to some damaged, broken old man who was never anything to you but a friend of your dad's? You would have... How was I supposed to do that?"

I breathe deeply, staring at a spot in the air for a long time. Hearing what he said. Understanding it. But also understanding the feeling of betrayal in my heart. "I see what you mean," I say at last. "It... It must have been really hard for you. I'm so sorry you had to go through it. I wish I could have... been there for you. But you've had weeks. *Weeks*. We've been getting closer all this time. Surely there have been plenty of opportunities for you to tell me between the hospital and now."

"I was—" He breaks off his own words. Doesn't complete them.

"You were scared."

"Yes. I was scared I would lose you a second time. I didn't think I could live through it again." His words aren't loud or emotional. They're quiet. As gentle as he's always been with me.

"You said earlier, after lunch, that you didn't want to make the mistake you made before and not tell me how you felt. Were you talking about a mistake you made with me before?"

"Y-yes. I almost lost you because I was afraid of sharing all of myself with you. I had trouble trusting that you could really... really love me, so I wouldn't make myself vulnerable. I wasn't going to do that again."

I swallow hard. Tighten my fingers into fists before I

purposefully release them. "But you did. You *did*. You did it again, Arthur. That's exactly what you did. You were afraid of telling me the truth about our relationship because you thought I would reject you. I understand that. I really do. And I can maybe get behind breaking it to me slowly. But you let me fall in love with you again—you watched it happen step by step—all the while lying to me about—"

"I didn't lie."

"Yes, you did. Maybe not directly. Maybe not in words. But everything you didn't tell me was a lie. That's how it feels to me. And you did it because you didn't trust me. You still..." I have to cough as a sob is trapped in my throat. "You still don't trust me."

"Baby, please—"

"I think I need some space." I blurt out the words because it feels like I'm drowning and he's coming closer. He's going to put his arms around me. He's going to hold me, make me feel better.

And I want it so much.

He jerks to a stop at my words. His face is twisted with emotion. "Wh-what?"

"Space. I need some space. I'm so confused and so upset, and I need to sort things out in my head."

"Yes. Of course you do. But maybe I can help you do that."

"No, you can't. You'll confuse me even more because I want you so much. I need to do this on my own."

"Baby, please don't push me away."

"I... I have to. For right now. We can talk again, but not yet. You said you want to give me anything I need, and I need this. I need space."

There's an internal struggle on his face for a minute until he gets control of it. "All right. I can... I can give you space. How much do you need?"

"I don't know. I really don't. At least a couple of hours."

"Okay. I'll be in my office. Come find me when you're ready to see me again."

His voice is absolutely heartbroken. I can't see his face because he's turned to leave the library.

It's horrible. Horrible. I feel like a villain, breaking a man who's already been broken by the world in so many ways.

But I've been broken too, and I need to figure out how to put myself together again.

An hour later, I knock on Arthur's office door and ask if I can borrow a car.

I'm going to take Fred and drive to Charlotte to see Jenna.

I've never seen anything as bleak and frozen as the expression on Arthur's face as he nods mutely and goes to his desk to get me a set of car keys.

"Are you okay to drive?" he asks softly.

"Yes." Everything is like ice inside me. The details of the world are starkly defined, no detail blurred or masked.

"Are you... Are you leaving me?" His hand shakes slightly as he passes me the keys.

"I don't know."

"I'd like..." He clears his throat. "I hope we can talk again before you make any decisions."

"I know" is all I say.

It feels like a stranger inhabiting my body, saying those words, moving my body, making me leave.

"I'll figure out a way to get the car back to you."

"Just keep it for now," he says. "It's the red BMW. I don't need it. You can bring it back when you're ready."

"Okay."

We stand staring at each other.

I hate this. I hate myself. I hate everything about this moment. But I don't know how to get out of it.

"I love you, Scarlett," he says as I leave. "You were right. I was still afraid to trust. That's why I didn't tell you. I'm... It's the first time in my life I've ever tried to do it, but that's no excuse for breaking what we almost had. So I understand if you need to leave. I want you to... be strong, and you're being strong right now. I'm so proud of how far you've come. And no matter what you decide, I'm going to love you forever."

I gasp. Freeze. That image that cracked in my head

earlier in the library shatters completely—breaking into a thousand slivers and pieces.

The dark fog in my head lifts. There's no barrier left to protect me. All of it hits. All the memories. All of them at once. Filling my mind, overflowing every boundary, coalescing into a complete picture.

It's too much. Way too much.

The world darkens again—completely this time. And the last thing I remember is being unable to raise my arms to catch myself as I fall forward toward the floor.

I come back to consciousness aware of a slight headache.

Shifting my body slightly, I realize I'm in a bed. It must be morning. I hate waking up with a headache.

Baby.

The voice is disembodied, but I feel it in my chest. I *want* it. A little whimper catches in my throat at how much I want it.

"Scarlett, it's time to wake up."

This time I hear the words for real. A male voice. Low. Slightly raspy.

Beloved.

"That's right, baby. Come back to me."

I whimper again and make an attempt to open my eyes. My lids flicker but don't lift.

"Good girl. That's it. You can do it. Open your eyes."

I have to see the face that goes with that voice. I *need* it more than anything. I try again, this time managing a slit between my lashes. Even the small amount of light blinds me, so I squeeze them shut again.

"Scarlett, you can do it."

"I know I can do it," I mumble grumpily. "But it's bright and I don't want to."

There's a choked sound. Maybe a laugh. Maybe a sob. Then "Let me close the blinds and you can try it again."

I listen to some rustling in the room for a minute. "Okay. Try now."

I blink a few times. When the brightness isn't so painful, I open my eyes completely.

I'm in a hospital room—stark and soulless—and Arthur is sitting in a small chair beside the bed. With a frown, I say, "You should be sitting in that better chair in the corner."

"It's too far away from the bed."

"Then move it if you have to. That chair you're in is going to kill your back."

"My back is fine." He's smiling fondly and scanning my face at the same time.

"It's not going to be for long in that chair. You need to switch the chairs." I'm getting anxious because the chair looks so uncomfortable. How long has he been sitting there, leaning forward in that way he does when he's stressed? His back is going to go out again. "Arthur, please."

"All right." He gets up and scoots the small chair out of the way. "I'm doing it now. Please don't get so upset."

I relax as he drags the larger, more comfortable chair over into the place near the bed, moving the small one into the corner.

He sits back down in the better chair.

I let out a relieved exhale.

"I'm okay, Scarlett. You don't have to worry about me. You're the one in the hospital."

"I come here way too much."

"Yes, you do. After this, let's take a decades-long break from hospitals. My poor heart can't go through this again."

I reach out, fumbling until he takes my hand in both of his. "Are you okay?"

"I'm fine, baby. The only thing wrong with me is that I'm worried about you."

"Oh. Okay." I swallow. "I think I'm okay. I have a little headache."

"They said you might have hit your head again when you fell. They couldn't find a bump or red spot, so it couldn't have been too bad this time. It looked to me like you just fainted."

I wrinkle my head, trying to think back. I was in Arthur's office. I fell toward the floor, everything going black.

"What do you remember?" he asks softly.

"I think I did faint. That's what it felt like. I was being bombarded with so much all at the same time, and it was too much. Or something."

He waits for several seconds before murmuring, "What were you bombarded with?"

It coalesces in my mind. Two complete narratives. No longer separated by that swirling fog. No longer shattered into fragments and scattered to the dark corners of my mind.

They've been collected again like the pieces of a puzzle, snapped neatly back into place.

Telling my whole story.

I remember all of it.

I start to cry.

"Oh no, baby." He reaches out with one of his hands like he wants to hold me but withdraws before he does. Instead, he cradles my hand and lifts it up to his mouth, kissing the knuckles softly. "I'm so sorry. You remember what I did now? You know you were about to leave me?"

My body is shaking, and I'm contorting my face in an attempt to control the sobbing. When I can breathe, I choke out, "I remember everything."

"I'm so, so—" He breaks off, stiffening his back. "Wait, what? How much do you remember?"

"Everything." I fall into helpless tears again. "I remember everything."

"Those six months?"

"Yes. All of it. It's all come back to me now."

"Jesus Christ," he breathes. "Does your head hurt bad? I'll get the doctor in, and he can make sure there's not any damage from—"

"I feel fine. A little headache. I don't think there's any brain damage. It's all just... so much."

He's relaxed again, hugging my forearm toward his chest. "I can't even imagine."

"I..." I lick my dry lips. "I fell in love with you twice."

His face tightens. "Baby."

"I can feel every moment of both times."

"Is it terrible?"

"No. I just feel like I might... overflow." I make myself let out a long, slow breath, trying to get a handle on everything I'm feeling.

I love him so much. More than a human heart should be capable of. And now that I can remember the first time, I understand in razor-sharp detail what Arthur must have gone through. I can read every moment after I lost my memory through the lens of what he must have felt.

I start to cry again.

"Fuck it all," he mutters. "Please let me hold you." He reaches out for me again, this time pausing right before he touches me. I sit up and close the gap between us so he can wrap his arms around me in an awkward, edge-of-the-bed hug.

I don't care. I need him. I cry into his chest for a long time.

When I've finally gotten control of myself, he lets me go, and I recline back against the pillow. "How did you... how did you even get through it? You must have been hurt so badly when I couldn't remember how we fell in love."

He blinks in surprise but answers easily enough. "It was hard. But it wasn't your fault. It happened to you more than it happened to me."

"Sure, but still. All those times you needed me, and I wasn't there because I didn't know. I can't imagine how you even got through it."

"I was okay. I didn't fall apart, which frankly surprised even me. It helped that I could still be around you. And once you weren't treating me like a stranger, things got better for me. I was so sure..." He lets out a faint huff. "I was so sure you'd never fall in love with me a second time. I was convinced it was a weird fluke of circumstance and timing, and it could never be repeated. You can't even imagine how shocked I was when slowly you seemed to like me again, you wanted to spend time with me, you wanted to be close. And then you wanted to..." He shakes his head. "It felt like a miracle. That even after losing you the first time, I might actually get to be with you again."

"When did you... When did you start to think it could happen again?"

He smiles and picks up my hand once more. "That

evening on the couch when you fell asleep on top of me. I held you for almost an hour as you slept, and I suddenly had hope. Your losing those first six months was a huge hole in my heart, and it always would be. But I could suddenly see a path forward even if you never remembered. Maybe we could still be together."

I can see it all. His experience of every moment. And he still lied—he still hurt me—but it doesn't feel as much like a betrayal.

I have no idea what I would have done if I were in his place.

"You should still be angry with me," he says softly, as if he's reading my mind. He's meeting my eyes soberly. "I did feel trapped by nothing but bad options, but I did what I did out of fear. Of being rejected by you. Of your breaking my heart even more than it already was. What if you learned we were together and hated the idea of it? That felt like the most likely possibility, and I didn't think I could live through it. But I was thinking about me in that. Not about you."

I nod because I understand and agree with everything he's telling me. I'm not shocked and angry anymore, but it does still hurt that he held back the truth from me for so long.

We sit in silence for a long time. I have no idea what to say, how to take us past this aching impasse.

Finally he says, "I've been thinking about this a lot. I

was desperate before. Desperate with the fear of losing you. And it made me selfish. But when you fainted earlier today, I thought you were..." He makes a guttural sound. "I thought you might be gone. It was the worst moment of my life, but it helped to put things in perspective. I'm not going to be desperate again. I don't have much practice, but I think I'm strong enough to do what's really best for you without falling apart. And that's what I want. What's best for you and not just for me."

"I want what's best for you too," I whisper.

His expression cracks for a minute before he's able to continue. "What's best for me is for you to be strong and well and free—and not putting aside anything that's important for you just to be with me."

"But—"

"Just hear my suggestion first. I promise I'm not pushing you away. You said earlier that you need space, and I think that was real. You were planning to go to Jenna in Charlotte, so once you're well enough, why don't you still do that? You take some time for yourself. Rest and recover for as long as you need. Even get a job if you want one. Try to connect with your old friends."

It sounds so good in so many ways, but there's one huge piece that's missing. "But I want to be with you."

"We can still be together. We can talk as much as you want, and I can come visit you whenever you want to see me. We can still be together, but no pressure. For real this time. Not just an excuse on my part to avoid taking a risk. I love you, Scarlett. I'll love you for the rest of my life. But I really think—and I've always believed—that you need a little freedom and independence. And tying yourself to me out of love without ever getting the chance to be the person you want to be on your own is going to take some of that away from you."

My mouth wobbles. My fingers tremble. "But you need me."

"I'm really okay, baby. I do need you, but I can do this. I'm not going to fall apart while you do what you need to do. I want this—for you and for me. Of course I'd love to snatch you back right now and never let you go, but I don't think either one of us has to love in desperation anymore. We can love freely. We can trust each other to always be there even when it's hard. I love you enough to give you what you need."

Tears pool in my eyes but don't fall. "I love you that much too."

He jerks his head to the side like he's hit with sudden emotion. But he turns back to meet my eyes. "Then give me this. What I need right now is for you to take the space you need. And if you still feel the same about me afterward, we can spend the rest of our lives together."

"I'd... I'd like that." I smile at him, and he smiles back.

And for once it doesn't feel like I've lost anything at all.

Three months later, I check my hair for the fifth time in the vanity mirror of the small apartment I've been renting since I came to Charlotte. I stayed with Jenna for a few days, but she has a family and her own life, and she didn't need a guest in her house for so long. So I found a short-term rental in a cute part of town and have been enjoying it.

Jenna even got me a temporary job at her library. It's not the most exciting work—particularly after the work I've done on Arthur's books—but it feels like a normal life and gives me something to do and money for bills.

I've had a good time these three months. I feel like myself again—whole and well and standing on my own feet. Arthur was right that I needed them, and I love him for making it possible.

He and I talk almost every day—sometimes for hours —and he's come up twice so far to see me.

It doesn't feel like enough, and I've been excited about this weekend for days now. He's getting to town right now and can stay at least a few days.

Fred nuzzles at my feet. He's clearly picked up my energy and is excited about whatever is happening.

"He'll be here in a few minutes," I tell him. "I know you've missed him too."

Fred gives a little yap, panting up at me happily.

"I think... I mean, I'm going to see how I feel in the moment, but I'm pretty sure I'm going to tell him this weekend that I've had all the space I need."

Fred cocks his head as if he's trying to listen.

"I feel so much better. About everything. I think we both needed a little time, but I think that time is over. I don't like being so far away from him. I think we both need to go home and be with him soon."

Fred whimpers enthusiastically.

"So that's what I'm going to tell him today. Jenna believes it's the right time too, and she's a lot smarter than me. Arthur will be so happy."

I have absolutely no doubts about that. He's not said a word of complaint, and he never even asks about my time-line. He was dead serious about not wanting to pressure me. But he's been waiting. He wants me back.

And I want to be back with him too.

"Oh look, he's here," I say after checking my phone after a text alert. "He's coming up."

I go to open the front door of the apartment, telling Fred to stay rather than running out in the hall to greet any newcomers.

Arthur is taking the stairs two at a time. He's wind-blown and smiling and wearing a green oxford with brown trousers. He stops in the hall when he sees me in the door-way. "Hey, baby."

"Hi." Then I can't wait anymore. I throw myself into his arms.

He laughs and hugs me so tightly for a moment I'm afraid my ribs may crack.

I don't care. I need it. Need him. He murmurs that he loves me against my ear.

And I love him too. No doubts or confusions. No regrets. I fell in love with him twice, and now the scattered pieces of our love have at last been collected into this moment.

Which will finally begin our forever.

EPILOGUE

FOUR MONTHS LATER

ONE OF ARTHUR'S COUSINS IS A HANDSOME, SERIOUS MAN IN his midthirties named William. Like Arthur, he's intelligent, guarded, and reserved—not opening up easily and trusting only a very small circle—but unlike Arthur, he genuinely loves the business world and has worked hard to help Arthur restructure the Worthing companies he's been managing for several years.

I've met him briefly a couple of times over the past few months as he and Arthur finalize the changes, but it's been hard for me to really get a clear sense of the man. He's got the Worthing brown eyes and deep sense of responsibility, but I honestly can't tell if he has Arthur's kind heart.

Arthur says he's a good guy, and I have no reason not to trust him, but William's composure is as impenetrable as stone.

Even at the celebratory dinner after the final contracts are signed, he's polite and professional but not friendly. Arthur has softened and relaxed a lot over the past year as he's let go of a lot of his emotional baggage, and he comes across as a laid-back extrovert compared to William.

Fortunately, William's fiancée is lovely and polished but far more approachable. She's a stylish blonde named Amber, and she appears genuinely happy to meet us. She's the heir to the hundred-year-old Delacourte jewelry dynasty, which evidently consists more of reputation and skill than actual assets.

The marriage will be advantageous to the Worthings, as it will bring the Delacourte name and brand into our fold. But from what I've picked up from Arthur, it will also be advantageous to Amber since her family no longer has any money.

I was expecting a mostly practical relationship from the two of them and was honestly intrigued to see what such a union might look like. It's not what I expect.

As our dinner progresses, I'm more and more convinced that Amber is in love with him, and the only time I see any sort of softness in William's eyes is when he's looking at her.

Maybe Arthur was wrong in his cynical assumption that it's not a love match.

Or maybe they started as practical but fell in love along the way.

I'm thrilled with that idea and hard-pressed not to interrogate them about the ins and outs of their relationship. Instead, we talk about business, about travel, about wine, about books, and about jewelry. I have a good time, and I like Amber a lot.

But I still really want to know what's going on between her and William.

After we have dessert, I excuse myself for the restroom and ask if Amber wants to join me. She does.

Before I can start with my questioning, she gives me a little smile. "So you and Arthur..."

I blink, pushing open the restroom door. "What about us?"

"Tell me about you. How did you get together? I want to know everything!"

I can't help but giggle since she's clearly been in the same state of curiosity as me. She just beat me to the questioning.

"We're not that exciting."

"What? I can't believe that. He's way older than you for one thing, but I can clearly see it's not a superficial trophy-wife kind of thing. That man is crazy in love with you. I've never seen anything like it."

I gulp and blush, taking the opportunity to close the stall door to hide my expression. "Uh, yeah, we're really in love."

"So how did you even meet him?"

"He... Well, to tell you the truth, he was a friend of my dad's."

She's clearly thrilled with this piece of information if her response in the other stall is any indication.

"But it wasn't creepy. There isn't a power imbalance or anything. We need each other equally."

"So how did it happen?"

I give her a brief rundown of my history with Arthur, concluding as we're washing our hands.

"But you're not engaged yet?" she asks, carefully pulling a paper towel from the holder.

I shake my head. "I wouldn't be surprised if it happens soon, but he hasn't asked me yet. We had a lot of stuff to work out, but things are going great now. I got a job at a university library, and he's going to start graduate school in philosophy in the fall. It's like we've both had a brand-new start."

"That sounds amazing. I'm glad you've worked things out. Relationships can be complicated." She's been looking me in the eye, actively listening, but now her gaze slips to the side like she's been hit with her own thoughts.

"They can be," I say slowly. "So tell me about you and William."

"It's... complicated."

"In what way?"

She throws away her wadded paper towel and stares at herself in the mirror. "I'm not sure if I can explain it."

"Try."

"I'm..." She gulps. "It started kind of... superficially between us."

This confirms Arthur's impression, so I nod.

"But now I'm crazy about him."

"What's wrong with that? He clearly isn't averse to you either."

"You think so?" It sounds like she doesn't even know.

"Of course. He's hard to read, but there's definitely something there. Have you not talked about it?"

"Uh, yeah. Kind of. But everything isn't sorted out. And..." Her face breaks briefly. "It's hard not to believe he wants someone other than me."

"I don't believe that." I'm not sure why I'm saying this. I know almost nothing about their relationship, and for all I know, Amber might be right. "But if you're worried about it, you need to talk to him again. Kind of talking isn't enough."

She makes a face at me.

"I'm not saying it will be easy. But you won't get what you need unless you do."

She gives a jerky kind of nod and then takes a deep

breath, visibly pulling herself together. "Sorry to dump that on you."

"You didn't dump anything. I asked. If you want to talk more, give me a call. The truth is, I can use some more friends."

Amber smiles, just slightly wobbly. "Me too."

The rest of our time together is pleasant and enjoyable, and I'm tired as Arthur and I return home to the Worthing estate.

Fred is waiting for us at the front door. He runs circles and wiggles and accepts pets and gives us a couple of reproachful yaps for deserting him so cruelly.

Arthur mentioned earlier that his back is bothering him a little, so I tell him to take a hot shower. I take off my cocktail dress and jewelry and put on a pretty gray night-gown, brushing out my hair in the mirror and wondering if the woman there is really me.

A year ago, I was living on the island with my dad, sad and lonely and miserable and completely isolated from life.

Now I'm here. With a life and a career and a dog and a future and a really good man I love.

Life always surprises you. And occasionally the surprises are good.

I'm still staring at myself in the mirror when Arthur gets out of the shower. His hair is wet, and he's wearing nothing but a pair of dark pajama pants. He comes up behind me and presses his front into my back, wrapping one arm around me.

"Hi," I say, smiling into the mirror at him.

"Hi." He's smiling with his eyes but not his mouth. It looks like he wants to say something. His other hand is behind his back for some reason.

I'm not sure why I notice that, but I do. "What is it?"

He opens his mouth but doesn't get it said immediately. Instead, he brings his hand around, showing me an open jeweler's box with something sparkling inside.

A ring. A beautiful diamond solitaire on an antique band.

I make a weird sound in my throat.

"I thought about doing something special and elaborate, but all my ideas didn't seem... right." His brown eyes are deep and soft and speaking, meeting mine in the mirror. "But I love you, Scarlett. I didn't expect it, and I still don't know how such a miracle happened to me, but I'm not going to let you go now that I've found you. You're already everything to me, and I hope you'll also be my wife."

I choke on a little sob, turning around in the circle of his arm and looking between the ring and his face.

His mouth turns up just slightly at the corners. "Do you have an answer for me?"

"Yes! The answer is yes!"

I throw myself against his chest, and he wraps both arms around me. After a minute, he pulls away and takes my hand so he can slide the ring on my finger.

We both stare down at it sappily.

Then I say, "I can't wait until we're married. Who else in the world will be able to say that they fell in love with their husband for the first time twice?"

ABOUT NOELLE ADAMS

Noelle handwrote her first romance novel in a spiral-bound notebook when she was twelve, and she hasn't stopped writing since. She has lived in eight different states and currently resides in Virginia, where she writes full time, reads any book she can get her hands on, and offers tribute to a very spoiled cocker spaniel.

She loves travel, art, history, and ice cream. After spending far too many years of her life in graduate school, she has decided to reorient her priorities and focus on writing contemporary romances. For more information, please check out her website: noelle-adams.com.

Made in the USA
Las Vegas, NV
16 February 2025

18216578R10152